TIME AFTER TIME

Lenore gave a delighted laugh at her daring reply. The man would be livid. Good! Feeling much better, she waited for the ink to dry, and then she closed the diary. She would send one of the servants to the Rose Tearoom with the journal. Before long the man would have it picked up and delivered to him. But the odd exchange was beginning to unsettle her, and once she received it back, she might burn the diary, get rid of it once and for all.

She went to the window and looked out at the street below. A servant walked a dog and an old woman hobbled along, swathed in a long gray cloak despite the warmth of the day. Lenore put her fingertips to her temple and rubbed. The memory of the kiss last night had awakened a longing for love, but she wondered if she would ever find someone who would not try to own her or belittle her in some way. Sighing, she touched her hand to her heart, knowing that at least she had peace if not love. The lonely yearning would recede with time.

She would surround herself with friends and dogs, and do without men forever.

DOUBLE DECEPTION

Maria Greene

ZEBRA BOOKS
Kensington Publishing Corp.
http://www.kensingtonbooks.com

Chapter 1

"The Rose Tearoom has been all the rage since Waterloo," Lady Blythe said to her grandson, who yawned. "Two sisters started the enterprise in conjunction with the Lythgow Hotel, and even the patronesses of Almack's frequent these premises at times. Their approval is what made this establishment a gathering spot for polite society."

"I daresay," Eric Ramsdell said and sent a jaundiced glance around the room, which was decorated with rose damask wall panels, rose-printed cloths on the tables, and a multitude of roses in vases adorning every flat spot in the large, sunny room.

Ladies of all shapes and ages occupied the tables, chatting away like macaws. He had little patience for it, but his grandmother liked to come for tea and cakes at times and who was he to refuse her wishes? She was one of the few people who really cared about him and who didn't give a fig for the *haute monde's* rejection of him. She understood him, and he understood her.

The old lady surveyed the gilt-edged plate of iced and sugared cakes placed in the middle of the table on a crocheted doily. She sipped her tea and dabbed at the corners of her lips with a napkin. "Try some ginger cake, m'dear. So good for the constitution."

He obeyed. Not that he really cared for ginger cake, but this one melted in his mouth, and the silver teapot wafted fragrant steam. The tea was excellent, and even if the display of lace and the profusion of flowers irked him, he had to admit the owners knew their customers' tastes. All the ladies he'd ever known liked fripperies and cluttered surroundings. He liked simplicity and clean surfaces.

His grandparents had inherited heavy pieces of baroque furniture, and he abhorred the exaggerated, gilded grandeur that filled every corner of the mansion in Berkely Square. At Swinmere, the Blythe estate, he'd rearranged the furniture more to his liking, and moved all ornate pieces into storage. His grandmother would not approve, but she rarely spent any time at Swinmere.

"You are very quiet, Eric. Is there something the matter?" She gave him a gimlet stare, and he squirmed inwardly.

"No, Grandmother, I'm just feeling somewhat out of place in this sea of overdressed females."

She chuckled and gave the room a cursory glance through her eyeglass. "You *are* the only male here today, except for the two servants. I would feel the same at one of your clubs. All those men staring at me over their claret bottles, all that somber leather and dark colors. Pah!" She leaned across the table and patted his hand with her pudgy one. "You are a very brave man to accompany me here."

He smiled. "Grandmother, I have faced much more frightening challenges in the past. A gaggle of giddy women does not intimidate me."

"Giddy gaggle indeed. Do not be so rude."

"I did not mean to offend you."

"Pshaw." She busied herself with a chocolate square covered with almonds and sugar glaze.

He looked across the plate heaped with cakes and weighed her words. His cynicism worried even him. How and when had life turned so tedious that he could see no distinction between one woman and another? They all seemed to speak in loud or fluttering voices, and their affectations only bored him.

He gazed across the room, dismayed at the frills and fal-lals of fashion that surrounded him, ruffles and ribbons, some more extravagant than others. The cost of keeping a lady in fripperies would be staggering.

Some of the ladies sent him simpering smiles and coy glances behind spread fans, and he fought an urge to get up, fling down his napkin in a show of disgust, and leave the room.

The only woman who seemed out of place, with her simple white gown and dark green velvet spencer, sat at a table at an angle to theirs. Three other ladies involved in an animated discussion shared tea with her. She wore no rouge and her black, lustrous hair had been fastened into a simple chignon that showed her long slim neck to advantage. Her face was framed by a dark green hat and her pale, flawless complexion almost had a pearly sheen; her profile, the strength and elegance of a Grecian marble bust. She must have felt his perusal because she turned her head and stared straight at him.

Her dark blue gaze glittered, piercing him to the marrow. No lady had ever stared at him so directly or so artlessly. Her self-possession took his breath away—and then she turned away as if she had only been interested in the wall behind him. He doubted she'd registered his presence.

She laughed at something one of the women said—he'd never heard a sweeter sound, melodious and clear. The day improved greatly with that sound.

He angled his head forward. "Grandmother, who are those women?" He indicated the table with his gaze, and she threw a quick glance over her majestic shoulder.

"Which one?" she asked. "You can't be interested in all of them."

"Why not?" He didn't want his grandmother to think he had a special interest in any one lady. Not that he did, but the stranger had sparked a faint light in the darkness of his soul. She was beautiful.

"The tall one is Mrs. Andrews, and the other, the blonde, is Mrs. Belinda Chandler, Sir Henry Sutton's daughter. The two others I do not know, but judging by their matronly looks, perhaps they are there to lend respectability to the situation. Their dress is most unconventional and they may be artists. As far as I know, Mrs. Andrews is a newcomer to London, spent years abroad. She has connections to the Colonies."

His spirits sank. "All married, eh?"

His grandmother rolled her cool blue eyes at him. "That would never stop you, Eric."

He didn't like the barb, but his grandmother was right. Nothing could change the reputation he'd acquired. "I suppose not."

She patted his hand across the table. "I could go on castigating you, but I do know how good your heart is. What's in the past shall remain there. No reason, surely, to dredge that up again."

"I'm grateful that you do not berate me in public, Grandmother," he said with a wry smile. "Everyone here would be all ears."

"Hmph." The old lady looked discreetly over at the other table. "I've heard Mrs. Andrews is a widow; she's barely out of mourning. Has been in Vienna for several years. It's commonly understood that Malcolm, the Marquess of Ludbank, is courting her. Everyone is astonished. After all, he could have anyone he wants."

"She must have made a deep impression on him."

"No one really knows. It's also said she won't encourage him, but he's very persistent."

"He's making a cake of himself, no doubt."

His grandmother clucked her tongue and patted the gray locks that surrounded her face under her bonnet. She gave him a long stare. "You never would, I gather." When he didn't reply, she continued. "I'd say you've never fallen in love."

"No, I have not, and I never will."

She studied him closely. "You have lost weight since I last saw you. Rusticating in Hampshire all by yourself is not healthy. You'll wither away to nothing if this goes on any longer."

"You prefer me to 'rusticate' in London, among those I offended? I think not."

"The Earl of Denbury is nothing to fear. He won't do anything—"

"He has done enough! He made sure I can't show myself in London for any length of time without repercussion. I'm reduced to eating iced cakes and drinking tea in ladies' tearooms."

"Fiddlesticks. You might not be invited to any gathering of the sticklers, but you're still a Ramsdell. When your grandfather dies, you'll be Viscount Blythe. You shall have to take your place in society."

"Denbury will hold a grudge for the rest of his life, mark my words."

"But it's over," Lady Blythe said with force. "He can't hold on to the past." She almost knocked over her teacup with an agitated wave of her hand.

He placed his hand on her arm. "Calm yourself, unless you wish to be the center of attention. You have been my staunchest champion, but you know that most others are giving me the cold shoulder, and will continue to do so."

"But you still have to take your place at some time, Eric. You can't turn into a country bumpkin; after all, you more than most enjoy the clamor of the capital."

"In my former life, perhaps. Now I prefer more quiet pursuits. Fishing and hunting are not as boring as I once thought, and I have gained a wealth of knowledge about managing Swinmere. It has enriched my life."

His grandmother seemed unconvinced, but she dropped the subject.

"I will, however, concede that it's good to be back in London."

"I knew it."

"The boxing establishments, the horse races, the cockfights, the hells," he said to tease her.

"The ballrooms, the soirées, the routs, from which you're banned," she countered with a sigh. "All those nubile young ladies waiting for the right gentlemen."

"I should thank my savior every day," he replied, and meant it as he viewed the nubile women in this very room.

"You will have to set up a nursery one day to forward our lineage."

"Plenty of time for that, surely."

"There has been a Blythe at Swinmere for the last five hundred years." She puffed herself up, an irate hen with a wobbling chin and ruffled feathers.

He shrugged his shoulders. There was no use arguing with his grandmother about this, a dispute he would never win.

He glanced at the lady in the white dress and the green spencer. The party was leaving and she stood up, willowy and quite tall—unfashionably tall in a world where short, blond, and blue-eyed nymphs held sway. She threw a quick glance at him as they passed his table, and again that instant connection stirred him deeply. She paid no attention to him.

They left on a wave of laughter and happy exclamations, though Mrs. Andrews remained silent. The air in the room deflated as she left, and he felt it keenly. He glanced across to where she'd been sitting and noticed a book bound with black leather on the floor under her chair. She must have forgotten it, he thought, his curiosity now roused.

He glanced toward the door to see if she was coming back, but there was no sign of her or any of the others. The maid brought the tray with empty dishes back to the kitchen, and without thinking, Eric got up and fetched the book, which he clamped under his arm. In passing, he said to his grandmother, "The ladies left something behind. I must return it to them." He hurried out onto the busy street, but there was no sign of the woman in the white dress.

He rifled through the pages of the book and found sloping handwriting on every page. It was a personal diary. He looked at the flyleaf and saw the name Lenore Andrews written in the same style. So it was hers—the thought excited him. Without thinking, he tucked it inside his tight coat, and returned to the tearoom. The scent of fresh, yeasty bread was tempting, and he found that his grandmother had ordered some more tea.

With a sigh of surrender, he sat down, his heart beating against the hardness of the book cover. Even if it was wrong, even if he violated the lady's privacy, he intended to read it. She would come back looking for it, no doubt, and he would return it on the morrow.

Yawning behind his hand, he sat through a lengthy enumeration of the childhood ailments of the offspring his cousin had fathered. Stephen and his wife had brought six into this world, though fortunately not at the same time. Eric was well versed about their lives, more so perhaps than Stephen himself. Grandmother knew everything that was happening in the family even though she rarely traveled.

And she had loyal spies among the servants. It was a sore subject that he didn't add more news to the gristmill, but he had added plenty in the past, and she would have to be content with that.

He finally brought his grandmother outside into the golden sunlight of the late afternoon. Just like him, she stood tall and proud. She was somewhat on the plump side, which added to her imposing appearance. She wore a dark blue dress and a cloak that enhanced the majesty of her figure.

Several of her acquaintances nodded to her in passing, but their attention slid over Eric, or they cut him directly. He was used to that, but he sensed that it bothered his grandmother, no matter how proudly she stood, and how stern her gaze if she disapproved of something. She detested the way her so-called friends ignored him, but there was nothing she could do.

"We must go home, Eric. Your grandfather will want

his supper at the usual hour. Heaven forfend we would be late for that."

"God forbid," he echoed. Lord Blythe was a man of fixed habits.

He greeted them affably as they stepped into the gloomy library where he spent most of his time while in London. He was a short man, gently spoken and mild in every way, in contrast to Lady Blythe. They complemented each other, or so everyone in the family said, and perhaps they did even if his lordship had to look up to gaze deeply into his wife's eyes. That suited Lady Blythe quite well.

They had been harmoniously married for fifty years, blessed late in life with a son and daughter when everyone thought the marriage would be barren.

Lady Blythe had stepped in to raise Eric after his mother died tragically in childbirth when he was three. Her newborn infant had died with her. Eric's father had been broken by his grief, and he'd died from a sudden fever when Eric was ten. Their loss had left a gaping hole in his life, which had never truly been filled.

"A game of chess after supper, Eric?" the viscount asked as he poured three glasses of sherry before dinner.

Eric nodded. He looked forward to beating his grandfather at the game, a rare occurrence, but he had been practicing at Swinmere.

Later that night, after a meal of crumbling fish in a lumpy white sauce, tough mutton, mealy potatoes, overcooked peas, and several games of chess, he retired to his bedchamber. Finally he would have a chance to read the journal.

He traced a fingertip over the name, following the

inky loops. Lenore Andrews. He quite liked the name;
it sounded solid and strong, with a dash of mystery.
Leonora was a more common name, and he wondered
why her parents had named her Lenore.

The name fit her, he thought. His heart started
pounding and a wave of guilt traveled through him as
he opened the diary. He silently called himself a
scoundrel for what he was about to do, but he
couldn't help himself. He began with the last entry,
which was yesterday, May 5, 1816.

> *I was beside myself this morning when I discovered
> that Ronald really was a spy, ferreting out the move-
> ments of that madman Napoleon. Certainly I can
> understand the necessity of keeping it a secret, but I be-
> lieved that all the time we were married I knew his
> business and took great interest in his diplomatic ser-
> vices. If not for him, I never would have met so many
> interesting people, or had such brilliant guests at our
> dinner table. What hurt the most was the fact that he
> had a secret life. I thought we shared everything inti-
> mately. He could have trusted me, and did not. I feel
> betrayed even if I can understand his reasoning. His
> mysterious disappearances, his evasions, his outright
> lies now make sense. The man whom I trusted with the
> minutest details of my life, held back a crushing
> amount of his.*

> *I feel as if I never knew him, the cheerful, the
> charming, helpful man behind the façade he presented
> to the world and to—myself! I am devastated to dis-
> cover that he maintained a mistress on the side—all
> part of his secret life. Why was I so naïve? Why didn't
> I see the signs? The man only married me for conve-
> nience, for the connections, for the possibility of*

advancement. Whatever he did for me was a sham, meant to pull me behind the light. Yes, Ronald had a diplomat's tact and perfect manners, but where was his heart? He had none!!! Only for that woman he kept on Gunter Strasse, but he deceived her as well, and their children. I almost faint as I think of the children he had—a boy and a girl, so cleverly hidden away. Did they know they were bastards? Perhaps he pulled them behind the light too?

We all deserved better, Ronald, you vile snake in the grass. What once was deep love has now turned into hatred and I shall never trust another man easily, because of your perfidy. How could you do this when I gave you everything? I trusted you, you cheat, and I loved you.

Eric looked up from the book, sensing her grief. The intimacy of the information made him uncomfortable. She would be distressed to know he was reading her journal like this, and he considered putting it down, but some perverse desire made him continue.

He opened the diary at the beginning. The first entry was two years ago. Evidently, she didn't write in it all the time. Her words bubbled with happiness.

Ronald brought me a large bouquet of red roses, and he had placed a poem about me in the middle, and a sapphire and pearl ring dangled on one leafy stem. Just as music flows through the city of Vienna, so flows happiness in my blood. I am so in love with this man even if my brother had misgivings about our marriage.

Despite Ronald's many years over mine, we are perfect for each other. I care nothing for what Edward says. Ronald knows me so well, and he anticipates my every wish.

Such innocence, Eric thought, disturbed. How many times had he seen that destroyed? His had been shattered long ago. It was the way of the world, but did it have to be? Probably. People invariably exchanged childlike trust for cunning. Someone who had once been a true friend could turn into an enemy when feelings were bruised.

He lay down on his bed, propping the feather pillows under his head and opened the journal at a random spot.

Men are beasts. They use everything and everyone for their own purposes. They crush women's tender feelings, and diminish their worth as individuals. They seem to lack the character to behave with any sensitivity to others. They are creatures who cannot think on their own, unless it benefits them in some way.

Eric put down the diary on the gold brocade coverlet beside him. Were gentlemen really that callous? To some extent she was right. Most of the older generation viewed females as little more than brood mares, and if they brought money to the union, so much the better. In important decisions, they had no say. His own generation had scarcely made any changes there, and as he looked back at his life, it was true enough that he'd used women for his own pleasures. It was commonplace; it was accepted behavior. He had always compensated the women for their services, and they'd been happy to take his money, or whatever bauble they'd coveted. Nothing wrong in that, surely. They knew what they wanted, and he knew what he wanted.

Had *he* done anything wrong?

Lenore was just lashing out in anger, but she ought to understand the ways of the world. Affairs weren't all kisses and roses, and love didn't always last. But one made arrangements, as his grandfather would have called them. Life went on.

He ought to tell her that. The journal contained mostly personal events and upheavals. She would be furious if she knew that her most intimate thoughts were at the moment propped up on his chest, all her fears and hopes revealed to his eyes.

He got up and sat down at the desk in the corner of his bedroom. Dipping his quill into the inkwell, he leafed through the pages to the last entry.

So full of judgment, he wrote. *If you were adequately taken care of in your marriage, I see no reason why you have to rebel against the common practices of this world. Gentlemen have maintained mistresses for as long as time itself, and to fight against that institution is foolish.*

You picture love as something all-consuming, with nothing hidden, nothing held back, but you have not discovered that gentlemen strive not for the same romantic perfection. We are content with harmony in everyday life, a willing and kind wife at our side, and successful rearing of children. Secrets serve a purpose if they protect someone from harm. In your case, it is unconceivable that your husband would share his professional confidences with you, something that would be a possible threat to England. I doubt that your husband could have done anything differently, no matter how much he disappointed you.

Truthfully, it probably distressed him greatly to keep things from you, but I rather suspect you will disagree with this. Do you?

He wanted to see if she would reply.

Her anger would certainly flare at this homily, but he spoke the truth, and she would have to see that— or not.

Anyway, he wouldn't have to worry about that. When she realized he'd read her journal, she would be furious.

A stab of guilt went through him as he thought of violating her privacy, but it had been well worth it. More than anything, it intrigued him to encounter a woman who had thoughts of her own, be they misguided or well founded.

That night he dreamed about her, black hair flowing down her back, the winds of freedom pushing her on as she ran across a meadow full of flowers. The sound of her laughter wove around him an enchanted web, and he hurried after her, only to find that she consisted of a wisp of fog.

That night, Mrs. Lenore Alice Andrews, *née* Brigham, tossed and turned, unable to find the peace of mind she sought. The fact that the diary had disappeared from the Rose Tearoom disturbed her no end. She'd returned there to retrieve it an hour after they had left, but none of the servants had seen it. One of the male servants had promised to contact her the moment it turned up, if it ever did.

Some stranger in London might even now be fingering her pages and reading with avid eyes. She cringed. She had not spared any of her emotions on the pages, but she'd never suspected that someone would witness her revelations. She might become the subject of gossip.

She flung the covers off as if suffocating from their weight. Why had she carried the satchel with her watercolor tools into the tearoom? How unnecessary. The diary had been among that paraphernalia, and she'd shown some of her flower studies to Belinda, whose passion was the art of watercolors. The diary must have fallen out as she lifted the overturned satchel from under her chair. Drat it!

She threw her arm over her eyes and sighed deeply. If only she could find a comfortable spot on this hard bed, but she never seemed to be comfortable anymore. Since Ronald died, her world had turned into a wasteland of unhappy revelations. Ronald had even fathered children out of wedlock with another woman, whereas he hadn't managed to produce any with her within the sanctuary of their marriage.

The sanctuary had turned out to be a cave without light, and she'd felt increasingly lost, her every step unsure.

She turned onto her side, looking at the dark shapes of her armoire and the two chairs on each side of it. This town house on Albemarle Street had never felt like home. Ronald had lived here before their marriage, and his presence seemed to linger in every piece of furniture and every scrap of linen. She had made no mark of her own, as they'd spent most of their married life abroad.

What had happened to the diary? She kept imagining scenarios, one worse than the next. What if someone printed it? Ronald had been a government representative, and had been privy to enough scandalous material to make fodder for the gossipmongers. No, that would never happen, she prayed.

Hot, she tossed some more. She didn't know what

she was doing here in London—just waiting for the days to pass. She hated it.

The hectic rounds of entertainment bored her due to their emptiness, and the restraints of society made her chafe at the bit like an impatient horse. Outdoors, in the parks or the countryside, she felt happier, less encumbered, and she chose to spend her time with friends who shared her taste.

As the clock chimed five, she fell into an uneasy sleep. In the morning she would return to the tea-room to find out if anyone had returned her journal.

"You are very fortunate, Mrs. Andrews," the owner's husband said at the Rose Tearoom when she walked in with Belinda. "Someone did indeed return your diary—someone's servant, that is—and we could not discover the name before he left, but the most important thing is that you've recovered your journal." He bowed from the waist and handed her the leather-bound book. Her heart pounded with relief as she accepted it.

"Thank you so much, Mr. Denton."

Tucking her diary under her arm, she turned to Belinda. "You don't know how much I worried."

Belinda nodded her curly blond head. "You don't need to be the center of attention. I'm glad the person who found it had the decency to return it."

"Yes . . . I wish I could express my thanks somehow." She entered the carriage behind Belinda. "Let us take the air in Green Park."

"Very good. I brought my easel, paint, and brushes," Belinda replied and adjusted her straw hat, with its wide pink ribbons tied under her chin.

"How is Adam this morning?" asked Lenore, knowing that Belinda's marriage to the self-absorbed Adam Chandler was not the easiest.

Belinda's lower lip trembled and a cloud crossed over her face. "He was ranting and raving as usual about the quality of the breakfast fare. I've had a word with Cook, but nothing changes. The truth is there's no problem with the food. It's Adam who always finds fault."

Lenore had a sinking feeling in her stomach, and she wished she could help Belinda, but the marriage had been doomed from the start. She knew Belinda had never had any tender feelings for her husband. Like so many, theirs was a marriage of convenience.

"It must be very difficult to live under those conditions," Lenore said.

"You learn to compensate, and you learn to keep silent. He can rant and rave all he wants, but he won't reach me. I live in my own world."

Lenore had many comments about Adam on the tip of her tongue, most of them derogatory, but she kept her mouth shut.

The sun slanted through the windows of the coach, brightening everything around them. As the trees of the park surrounded them, she smoothed down her gown of sprigged muslin, and looked at the diary in her lap. Idly, she flipped the pages and to her surprise, she noticed the boldly scrawled entry at the end of her own outpourings. She held her breath as she read the brief lines.

"Such presumption! The person who found the diary has written to me. Listen to this." She repeated the lines scribed in Ronald's defense, her voice rising with anger at every word.

"Obviously a male viewpoint," Belinda said, her lips turning downward. "Threat to England, indeed!"

"Why would a stranger feel entitled to lecture me about my outpourings in my most personal journal? What incredible gall!"

"I'm appalled he would write his opinion and then bring the book back to you," Belinda said. "'Tis the height of arrogance."

"And outright cruel," Lenore replied.

"A severe violation of your privacy."

"If I can find out the identity of this man, I shall give him a piece of my mind." Lenore flung her diary aside, and it slid to the floor of the coach.

"He's too cowardly to give you his name, and he's certainly not a gentleman."

"That's obvious. He's a cad of the first order." Lenore fumed in silence and wondered what kind of ogre dared to insult her so.

They arrived at their bucolic spot among a grove of trees in Green Park where they'd decided to put up their easels. They got out of the carriage and a brisk breeze tried to pull Lenore's bonnet off her head. She pushed it down more firmly as one of the lackeys brought her painting materials out and helped her to set up.

The wind played in the wide canopies of the elms above, and birds sang in the dancing shadows. Lenore wished she could better appreciate the idyllic scene, but she was still steaming over the journal. Belinda hurried across the parkland with her painting tools, leaving Lenore behind. She preferred to paint in privacy.

The sound of hooves came to Lenore's ears, and she looked automatically toward the lane. Two gentlemen had stopped their mounts and one lifted his hat in a greeting.

"Lenore! I'm not surprised to find you here on this most beautiful morning." Sir Charles Minion, one of her friends, gave her a warm smile, and she waved.

"But I am surprised to see you abroad so early," she replied. "You're always nursing a sore head in the morning."

He and the stranger dismounted and sauntered over. She didn't recognize the gentleman who accompanied Charles. He had piercing dark eyes and stood tall and haughty, his dark hair curling under his tall beaver hat. He had a magnetic attraction that made her curious, but she sensed a dangerous side to him, as if he were ready to jump at anything that provoked him. She had never seen a more handsome man, but she held that against him, as he was bound to be nothing more than a selfish boor.

Sir Charles smiled. "Lenore, meet my friend Eric Rams—"

"Enchanted, I'm sure," the stranger said, interrupting suddenly.

Sir Charles gave him a strange look.

Chapter 2

The stranger bowed, showing very little deference or interest in her, which took her aback. "Mrs. Andrews," he added. His voice held a deep resonance that stirred her. He didn't try to kiss her hand, but his penetrating dark gaze, which had seen too much in life, made her slightly uncomfortable. She had set eyes on him somewhere, but couldn't place him.

"Both Lenore and I have our roots in East Anglia, but she's been gone for so long, we almost lost our connection," Sir Charles explained. He turned to Lenore. "I know Eric from my school days. We didn't see each other for a long time when I traveled to the West Indies with my father. Eric has been away for some time, and has only recently returned to London."

"I see. You traveled to foreign parts, Mr. Ramsey?"

"No."

Silence hung uncomfortably between them, and he didn't elaborate.

"He's dedicated to his estate, Swinmere," Sir Charles continued.

"Ah, yes. I admire gentlemen who take interest in their land and their tenants' well-being. So many don't."

"Possibly," he replied. Silently he seemed to say, "I don't really care."

She had expected him to smile at her compliment, but no emotion crossed his face, except for the deep glitter in his eyes. Did he have any kind of personality? She wondered if he could sense her discomfort, but she hoped he could not. Usually, she had no problem with self-confidence, rather the contrary, according to Ronald. He had called her "forward" and "disrespectful" when she spoke her opinion. He always said it with a smooth smile, but the underlying barb had poked through.

"I had a rather disturbing experience on my way here." She told them about her diary and the scathing entry at the end. "It infuriates me that someone would take it upon himself to judge my most private writings."

"How uncouth indeed," Sir Charles said, his forehead furrowed. "Do you want me to look into it for you? Someone must know who returned your book. A public building like that has ears and eyes everywhere."

"I did not think of that when I retrieved the journal. Oh, I'm still fuming."

Mr. Ramsey spoke, "Perhaps the gentleman in question had some valid points? Sometimes we don't see our own shortcomings, and cannot move forward. Your current anger would certainly indicate that."

Smoldering, she stared long and hard at him. "Sir, you don't know what is involved in this matter. Please refrain—"

"The truth can be upsetting at times, and perhaps you don't like the truth."

She couldn't believe she'd heard right. "So—you choose to defend the stranger's side, a man who violated me, without really knowing what it's all about?"

Sir Charles eyed his friend closely and slapped him

hard on the shoulder. "I doubt Eric means any of those statements. He always likes a heated debate and hopes to provoke people to think about what they're saying."

Lenore stared at the stranger, anger coursing through her. "No need to defend him, Charlie. I am sure he can speak for himself."

Mr. Ramsey bowed. "Thank you for having so much confidence in me."

Lenore straightened her back and mustered all the pluck she could find. "I take umbrage at your cynicism, and I don't even know you, Mr. Ramsey."

"I believe there's more than one side to every picture, so if someone stands firm on one point, I have to challenge it." He paused, his gaze searching hers. "Have you ever tried to step into someone else's shoes, tried to discover what it's like?"

"I do not understand your implication."

"Then perhaps you do not know what it means to be an outcast, or different. I find my peers rather stiff-necked, no insult intended." He placed his hands on his back and stared at her openly.

She could not detect any challenge in his eyes, which somewhat deflated her own defense. She'd never heard anyone speak so frankly, and had no idea what to say in return.

"Your easel has blown over," the stranger said as she floundered.

"Oh."

At least he wasn't prone to useless flowery compliments, she thought, something she appreciated. "Thank you, I'm sure the servant will take care of it." She threw a glance at the man scurrying to pick up some loose sheets the wind had scattered.

"He missed some."

The stranger's a complete boor, she thought, *one prone to find faults with everything and everyone.* She disliked people like that, but then again, she disliked most things in her life at the moment.

To her surprise, the gentleman hurried over to pick up her artistic endeavors from the ground before they blew into the pond beyond. He studied her efforts, one after the other. "He seems rather remote," she whispered to Sir Charles. "Does he have a sense of humor at all?"

Sir Charles laughed. "When he wants to. I have rarely seen anything ruffle his demeanor. He's wholly in command of himself."

"I'm surprised he would bother pick up my efforts at art."

"Eric will surprise you, but one thing I know, if he didn't want to pick up your paintings, he wouldn't."

She crossed her arms over her chest and looked up into his kind face. Tired lines pulled his lips downward. "How are things progressing with the fair Davina Bright?"

He sighed theatrically. "The jewel of my eyes has no patience whatsoever for me. I make a cake of myself at her feet, and she gives me a cold shoulder or a toss of her fair head."

Lenore clucked her tongue. "I've tried to intervene for you, but she's as flighty as a butterfly."

"And changes admirers by the dozen. She collects them as if she has an insatiable desire for victims. Broken hearts line her path."

"You talk about her as if she were a man-eating monster."

"She is," he said with a shrug of his shoulders. "I am resigned to always pine for her, the fairest of the fair."

"Do not let your heart break in the process."

"I shall pine until there's nothing left of me."

"Balderdash."

The stranger walked toward them. He had lost his hat and the servant retrieved it. The disarray of his dark, wavy hair made him look less severe, but she sensed the steel of power as he moved across the grass. She smiled at him tentatively, and he quirked his lips as if he didn't know how to smile back. Lenore would not want him as an adversary—come to think of it, she would not want him in her life.

"Thank you," she said simply as he joined them. "Very thoughtful of you."

She expected a smile then, but could detect no softness stealing across his features.

"You show fair talent," he said simply. "I can understand why you pursue such pastimes. I dabble in writing myself."

"Vicious editorials, no doubt," she said before she could stop the words from tumbling out.

Now his lips quirked upward. "Yes . . . anything critical or provoking. I cannot resist stirring the pot."

"Well then, perhaps people are writing about *you*?"

"It's possible." An unholy light began to smolder in his eyes. "All that is scandalous, in fact."

"You have put me in my place," she murmured, feeling the heat in her cheeks.

"No, I do not speak in jest."

Now she was both intrigued and even more mortified. She'd spoken as if implying she knew about some scandal in which he'd been involved. Words could carry you down a swift and dangerous river. She knew that all too well, thanks to her careless, impulsive nature. "It is truly a beautiful day for watercoloring," she said, clinging madly to the river's edge.

He suddenly smiled. She had never felt so awkward since she was five and told her uncle that his nose turned purple when he laughed. This encounter was not going well. Besides, why did his presence make her heart flutter? Troubled, she turned to Sir Charles.

"How is your mother?"

"Rather the same. Nothing can soften that iron will of hers." He elbowed Mr. Ramsey in the ribs. "Remember when we went riding as boys without her permission?"

Mr. Ramsey chuckled. "I could not sit for a week after the punishment."

"And we had to muck out the stables for a fortnight. Mother always has a way of making her point."

"Yes, you never made the same mistake twice."

"Perhaps she was strict because your father died so young," Lenore pointed out. She turned to the stranger as she felt his gaze resting on her. Self-conscious, she fingered the lace fichu at her neck, but it lay as perfectly as she'd arranged it this morning. "What about your parents?"

"Both gone for a long time, alas. My grandparents stepped in and did their best to make a gentleman out of me. I'm afraid, however, that I've been a sore disappointment to them."

Again he was hinting at a life that was less than exemplary. The mystery surrounding him intrigued her, but she was careful not to say something provoking. She gave him a smile. "I'm sorry to hear that. I understand, because my parents both passed on too. I know what grief is. Not too long ago I lost my youngest brother. I have come to accept that loss, but my other brother, Edward, never has. They were close."

Sir Charles got a look of panic on his face, and she wondered what had triggered it. Just as she opened her mouth to ask him, he took Mr. Ramsey's arm. "This is much too morbid for me. Let's ride back into the thick of things, old fellow."

Mr. Ramsey shrugged as if he didn't care, and Lenore silently wondered at Charlie's obvious distress. He bent over her hand. "I'm sorry, m'dear, but I just recalled a pressing engagement."

"Not with the fair Davina, I take it?"

He shook his head, a pined expression on his face. "Definitely not."

She slapped his arm gently. "Don't make a cake out of yourself or you'll regret it."

"I shall remain strong, but it's difficult."

She watched them leave after Mr. Ramsey had given her a curt bow. The turnabout in Sir Charles's demeanor puzzled her no end. Oh well, he was unpredictable at best, but a good man, nevertheless.

There were few of those, and he deserved better than Miss Davina Bright.

She stepped across the parkland and spotted Belinda in the distance by the pond. Her friend hadn't bothered with civilities. When she had a chance to paint, nothing could stand in her way. She glanced up at Lenore, her brush poised. "Who was that?"

"Sir Charles and a rather unpleasant friend of his. No one who would interest you."

Belinda didn't reply. Lenore sat down at her easel some distance away and wondered if she would ever feel any kind of inspiration again. She rummaged around in her satchel for her brushes and came across her diary again. The servant must have put it back inside. She flinched away from it as she recalled the violation of the stranger, but anger grew within her as she thought of his comments. To relieve her ire, she retrieved a case containing a goose quill and ink, opened the journal and started to write a reply:

It is obvious to me you're a gentleman of small consideration, if a gentleman at all. 'Tis evident you have some schooling, which separates you from a less fortunate segment of the population, but in some ways you're much more uncouth than our friendly street sweeper. That you would violate my privacy and read my diary, let alone write derogatory comments in it, *is totally beyond the pale.*

Clearly, you have no understanding at all of the importance of honesty. It is evident in your shallow comments that your viewpoint is male—and that the deeper regions of the human heart are unknown to you.

To maintain that a husband keeping a mistress is quite natural shows a superficial understanding of the true state of matrimony. Without trust, there is no union of souls. Why marry in the first place? Marriage is not merely a social institution, nor is it a convenience.

Your opinions are conventional, unconcerned with the actual meaning of the holy union promised in front of God at the altar. Not that someone like you would approach the altar in the first place, as it means you would have to think about someone else besides yourself.

Your scathing reply in the face of my misery as I try to deal with the knowledge of my husband's perfidy is heartless and outright ignorant. I understand that he would keep the nature of his work a secret to protect me, but again, it is essentially dishonest, and without hon-

esty, you have nothing. You call my romantic "notions" misguided, but a lady has the right to know whom she's marrying. However, I blame myself for my ignorance about such matters. But he confounded my perception with smoke and mirrors, and I can find no excuse for that.

She felt better for venting her anger on paper, yet anger still lingered at the gall of the stranger who had challenged her thinking. Nothing altered the fact that Ronald had not been the man she had thought.

Sadness overcame her, but she fought it. Ronald had already robbed too much of her life and she had to move forward, though the stranger's comments brought back the pain of the past.

She wished she could regain the high spirits of her innocent youth, but they were hidden under layers of disappointment. Her friends and acquaintances looked at her with pity, as she had no children to console her, despite the failure of her marriage, but she didn't worry. She would never want any children of hers to grow up without a father.

"You look very serious," Belinda said, cutting into her thoughts.

"I've been pondering my life. Surely it's better to live in harmony with oneself and alone than in a miserable marriage."

Belinda didn't respond, and Lenore could have kicked herself for bringing up the issue. Sometimes she forgot Belinda's circumstances.

She continued. "Life is like bubbles on a pond, glittering and traveling lightly over the water, but they are easily pierced and then nothing remains except the water, murky and cold."

Belinda sighed, putting down her painting tools. "That's an odd observation, but I daresay you're right. We are filled with hopes until reality pierces those hopes, and then we make the best of it."

"If we didn't have hopes, how would we dare to move from youth into adulthood?" Lenore pointed out.

"Not everyone experiences disappointment in marriage," Belinda said.

"That's true. You're the bravest person I know, Belinda. Despite the disillusionment you've experienced, you remain composed."

"You learn to compromise, and I appreciate my friends more. Without you, life would not be the same."

Lenore laughed, pleased, yet upset at the truth of it all. "We sound excessively grim," she said.

Belinda returned her attention to her painting. "I can't seem to find my inspiration today. My brushstrokes have all the subtlety of two left-handed monkeys."

Lenore laughed and tilted her head back. The wind tried to tear her hat off, but she held on to the crown. She almost toppled from her stool and her diary fell from her lap. "At least you haven't lost your sense of humor."

Belinda shrugged. "If you lose that, there's truly no hope left."

"We ought to do something wildly improper to entertain ourselves," Lenore said.

"Like drinking several bottles of champagne in broad daylight?"

"Why not? It's not a bad idea." Lenore called the lackeys with a wave of her hand and asked that their picnic be set up. One servant filled two glasses with the sparkling wine.

Belinda stared wild-eyed. "You actually brought some?"

"No crime in that, surely. We can always celebrate our health and—oh, our artistic ability. Besides, we are no simpering debutantes; we have a modicum of freedom."

Belinda giggled and they toasted their fortune. "As long as Adam doesn't find out and forbid me to see you." She sipped her wine and picked up the diary. "What did you write?"

Lenore showed her the pages, and her friend read. "This is excellent. You ought to bring the book back to the Rose Tearoom and leave it there for him to see. After all, he ended his entry with a question, so most likely he expects a reply." She pointed to Lenore's writing. "This ought to give him his comeuppance."

"Yes . . ." Lenore thought about it. "I would have preferred to say it to his face, but since we don't know his identity, there's no chance of that."

"Unless we park ourselves there for hours and spy on the guests." Belinda frowned. "The only flaw is that he might not be the one to pick it up."

"That's a possibility, but I daresay he will look for it. Besides, if someone else finds it, I'm sure they'll return it to the staff. Most people are not like this perfidious stranger who likes to pry."

"You may be right. But do you want to take the chance?"

"I might. I would dearly like to watch his expression as he reads my entry."

"That's not likely to happen."

Lenore made a *moue*. "You're right, but at least I've given him back some of his own vitriol."

Chapter 3

Eric had been surprised when Charlie invited him to ride in the park. They had been friends more years than he could remember, but did not see each other often. Then he'd found out that Charlie wanted inspiration on how to court the woman of his dreams, the toast of the *ton,* the fair Davina. Disgusted, Eric had suggested that Charlie look in a different direction for a wife, but the man was smitten. He wouldn't hear any criticisms toward his beloved, even if Davina was both spoiled and overbearing.

Encountering Mrs. Andrews and her friend in Green Park had taken Eric aback. All he could think of was the diary, and her anger at the stranger's—*his*—opinion that he'd written there. Mrs. Andrews had indisputable beauty, with her dark hair and sparkling eyes. She had touched him in a deeper way than he cared to admit with her frank approach and her vitality. He wondered if she would return the diary to the Rose Tearoom with a scathing reply for him.

He rather hoped so.

His grandmother looked at him in surprise when he suggested they repair to that establishment for refreshments on the following day.

She complied. "I must say I never expected this

turn of events," she said when seated in front of a table filled with iced cakes and a tea service. "I thought you abhorred this place."

"I do," he said, "but I enjoy your company, Grandmother."

"Pshaw. I do not believe such blandishments, but I admit I like the sound of them," she said with a pleased smile.

He looked all around the room, but saw no one remotely resembling Mrs. Andrews and her bold beauty. Insipid pinks and creams predominated among the dresses of ladies present, and he found himself getting bored very quickly.

There was always a chance Mrs. Andrews would appear, and then she would suspect him of writing the secret entry in her diary, but to his relief, he noted two other gentlemen present in the room, both mirroring his own expression of boredom.

"I don't know why you even bother, Eric. Am I your last resort? It's not as if I *need* your company. I could ask any number of my friends to accompany me here."

He opened his mouth to protest, but she interrupted. "And don't lie to me. There's no reason for pretense."

He shut his mouth and sighed.

"What you need is some more entertaining in the circle of your own friends," she said. "You will go totty-headed before your time if you keep cloistering yourself at Swinmere for much longer."

He nodded. "We have gone over this before, but I shall contrive to entertain myself. The inspiration has not been there for something else, Grandmother."

"Yes . . . I understand that. It's very hard to lose a

friend to death, but it's all in the course of nature. You have to continue. Life moves on relentlessly."

He nodded. He had heard the lecture before, but it didn't make the future any easier.

"I hear Sir Charles Minion is in town," she continued. "He should be able to bring you out of your doldrums."

"Yes, but I don't need his help, Grandmother."

She wagged her finger at him. "You are incredibly stubborn. But you agree with everything I say, and then go about doing as you wish."

He chuckled. "I daresay no harm has come of it, and I'm no longer in short coats."

"It's always hard to bridge an old life to a new. Your debauchery led you nowhere, so where do you go now?"

"Into boredom," he said, more to himself than to her.

"What?"

"Into a bright new world," he said mechanically.

"I worry about you," she replied after a long pause.

He realized Mrs. Andrews would not show up, and he saw no sign of her diary. Perhaps it had been presumptuous of him to think that she would return his correspondence. Fifteen minutes later, he assisted his grandmother with her shawl and her parasol, as they got ready to leave. Throwing a hopeful glance at the door, he knew in his heart he would not encounter the widow.

On his way out, he noticed a dark leather-bound book on the sideboard where the servants kept clean china and trays. It had been shoved partially behind a tall flower urn, and his heartbeat escalated as he recognized the volume. Mrs. Andrews had indeed left the diary, and he knew it would contain a return correspondence. As his grandmother greeted a friend, he quietly slipped the book under his arm and went toward the door. He couldn't wait to get home and read what she'd written.

She called him uncouth and ungentlemanly. He laughed, and felt that she was right, and yet, it galled him. He could be uncouth when it suited him, but he was fair. It never occurred to him to be unpleasant for no good reason—something he would point out in the diary.

Her life intrigued him. He opened the diary at random and found another entry.

> *I worry about Edward, who has no one but me to comfort him in his grief. I feel helpless as I see him suffer, and I wish he had a wife at his side. He needs someone to enliven that mausoleum he calls home. It is not my place to change it though I wish sometimes to bring some feminine touches to brighten up the house. Ronald's town house has similar flaws. It ought to be sold, as I never felt at home here. Ronald's indifference to my discomfort only makes it worse.*

Why had Mrs. Andrews felt out of place in her own home? Her husband had been callous not to heed her uneasiness. He started writing:

> *Clearly yours was not a marriage made in heaven. They rarely are, as we discussed earlier. Even though I've never spoken with Mr. Andrews, I can see he had no understanding of your needs. You call me callous and uncouth, and perhaps I am, but I've always been aware of others' feelings. If I have one weakness it is*

to put others' welfare before my own. That, however, does not have any bearing on my opinions about what you describe as the "holy bond of matrimony." True enough, I have no experience with those holy bonds, but neither do you, however much you take it upon yourself to judge such things. Your marriage was hardly a "holy bond" if there was another woman involved.

I can understand your bitterness, but not all gentlemen behave as your husband did. You cannot rake everyone over the coals and not expect resistance.

He put his quill down and stared across the room where dust motes danced in a beam of sunlight streaming through the window. He sighed, tired of his own restricted circumstances. But as he thought of the things available to him, a sense of fatigue came over him. How stifling it was to bring back the memories of his erstwhile carefree life.

He couldn't go back to the past.

Unable to write anymore, or to read more tidbits about this woman who intrigued him, he decided to go for a ride. Damn the fashionable hour in Hyde Park. He would try some less public places for his exercise and visit some alehouses along the way.

As he rode onto Berkely Street, he encountered Charles Minion, who looked happy to see him and acted as if in a hurry. "Eric, old fellow. Just the man I wanted to see."

Eric reined in his tawny gelding. "What's the urgency?"

"I know you're not busy tonight."

Eric shrugged. "You need little intelligence to figure that out."

"Go with me to Vauxhall tonight. No one will

recognize you in the dark—not that it would matter—but we can get a table at the back."

Eric thought for a moment.

"Don't dare to turn me down. I want you to see the fair Davina so that you understand my predicament."

"I shall *never* understand the depth of your weakness, but I daresay it would be an entertaining way to spend the evening."

Charles lit up. "You won't regret it, and be careful about what you say. Next we know you'll be in the throes of a consuming passion."

Eric looked askance. "Hardly likely. I'm not capable of it."

Charles laughed derisively. "That's what I thought too, until Cupid's arrow struck me without mercy."

"Yes, blame it on someone else." Disgust laced Eric's voice. "You nauseate me, you know."

Charles laughed again and bowed with mock humility. "I shall remove my humble person. Heaven forfend that I would upset you in any way."

"You're doing it too brown, Charlie." Eric wheeled his horse around. "Just be prepared. Your sterling reputation might be tarnished if you are seen in my company."

"I'll survive. I'm never bored in your company."

"I'm not the man I once was. I'm disgustingly boring these days."

Charles looked at him hard. "Boring? Never. Do you remember when we climbed into some young damsel's window those years ago?"

"And almost got shot in the process. Her father was livid. Fortunately he did not discover our identity."

"That didn't stop us from further antics. Where did

our sense of adventure go?" Charles shook his head in wonderment.

"We grew older, my friend." Eric had enjoyed his escapades, but he didn't have any desire to return to those days. "And we have evaded parson's mousetrap until this day. That's a feat in itself."

Charles laughed. "You shall not get a medal for it."

They rode through the noisy streets, where vendors of newssheets and flowers hawked their wares. Alluring aromas from the meat pie stalls wafted through the air, competing with the more pungent odor of horses and coal stoves. The sun played among cottony clouds and Eric felt a lifting of his spirits as he gazed heavenward.

"Perhaps it sounds odd, but I don't mind the idea of getting leg-shackled," Charles continued. "I have to look toward the future of Brookston. The estate needs the continuity of the family. The patter of tiny feet."

"You sound just like my grandmother. She wants those heirs to Swinmere. Heaven forfend that it would descend to some 'upstart' cousin. I am the only true Blythe heir—to quote her pompous words."

"And that's the truth, and you can't very well install a demirep on the premises."

Eric chuckled. "And what would be so bad about that?"

Charles tapped his crop on Eric's arm. "Nothing to joke about. I've heard horror stories about such arrangements."

"I never knew you to be narrow-minded, Charlie."

"No, but I would not want to put everyone at Brookston into an uncomfortable situation."

"Yes, I see your point. I believe, however, that we are bound by too many conventions. There's no room for change. You have to tread the same path as your forebears, and if they married advantageously, you are expected to do the same."

Charles nodded. "Of course. But we shall have to take care not to become as conservative as our parents. Do you remember how we scoffed at tradition when we were greenhorns?"

"Well, we certainly sowed our wild oats. The emphasis is on 'wild,' of course."

Charles grinned. "Indeed."

That night Eric looked forward to joining his friend at Vauxhall Gardens. Charles had reserved a supper box by the Grove, and sat there by a younger man with carefully arranged and pomaded brown hair, wearing a coat much too wide for his shoulders. Eric approached at nine o'clock. The popinjay could not hide his youth with his affected style.

"Eric, this is Ricky Monford, my cousin Anne's oldest son."

Eric shook hands with the young man, noting the intelligent twinkle in his eyes. "Pleased to make your acquaintance, Ricky."

"I requested a supper of ham and cutlets for ten o'clock." Charlie indicated a bottle on the table. "Have some of this excellent claret."

Eric joined his friend and looked around the Grove. Muted lights lit the other supper boxes, and he could make out some of the paintings of ruins and Greek gods that adorned the walls. He recognized a great many people, but none who would want to acknowledge his presence. In fact, he noticed furtive looks in his direction, and whispers behind gloves and spread fans. He didn't care.

The ladies looked beautiful in their jewel-hued evening dresses and glittering gems; and the more soberly dressed gentlemen either kept a proper bored countenance, or held the look of prowling predators as they viewed the daring décolletage of the ladies' attire. At Vauxhall, anything could happen under the Chinese lanterns and along the dark walks that crisscrossed the gardens. Illicit lovers could find a secluded spot for passionate kissing, or more. Young slyboots could find a way in the dark to slip forbidden billets to the strictly chaperoned damsels they admired.

"Cheers, old fellow," Charlie toasted. "To your freedom. To new beginnings."

Eric smiled, pleased. "Thank you." He pondered Charlie's words and felt a sense of lightness, as if a new wind had blown into his life. As he took a sip of the claret, he began to relax. This could prove to be an interesting night.

The orchestra played with passion, something by Handel, and Eric leaned back, watching the people milling back and forth.

As they enjoyed the food later, and a bottle of champagne, Eric noticed a tall, dark woman on the path bordering the boxes. She was laughing at something her gentleman partner said. He could have recognized that rippling laugh anywhere. Lenore, Mrs. Andrews. Her escort was Lord Ludbank, and Eric felt a strange sense of discomfort. The man stood proud and tall, and as he leaned toward Mrs. Andrews, their dark heads nearly touched. They seemed made for each other. Among his peers, Ludbank was known for his flamboyant character, his volatile temper, and his bouts of reckless gambling. He loved courting women, and Eric had to admit he was surprised when he heard the marquess had fixed his interest on Mrs. Andrews. She was far from the toast of the *ton,* and her widowhood at a young age set her apart. None of that seemed to influence the marquess. He kissed her hand as he held it protectively in his.

Two other women joined them, and Eric recognized her companions from the tearoom. They all looked rather inebriated, but it could just be simple enjoyment as more laughter rose at a joke Ludbank delivered.

Mrs. Andrews's gaze landed on Eric as the marquess whispered something in her ear, his face turned sideways. She recognized Eric and her eyes narrowed as if to better comprehend his expression. He gave a curt nod.

"Lenore!" Charlie shouted, raising his glass. "Do join us for champagne."

Eric stiffened, his fingers clenching around the wineglass, and his heart jolted uncomfortably in his chest.

"Sir Charles," she greeted, moving forward, her hand still clasped in Ludbank's.

Ludbank gave the scene a cursory glance and offered the men a nod. *He must not recognize me in this dim light,* Eric thought. Thank God.

"We are meeting a group of people later, but you can always join us when you're finished. Davina will be there." She kept talking, but a crescendo in the music drowned out her voice.

Charlie waved and nodded as the party moved off. "Isn't she beautiful?"

Eric nodded. "Yes, I must admit she has an abundance of elegance. Not my style, though. She, lacks in feminine charm."

Charlie groaned. "You barely know her."

"You have a point. I apologize for my crusty behavior." Fatigue overcame him and he wondered where his enjoyment had gone. Seeing Mrs. Andrews so closely attached to Ludbank had flattened his wave of happiness.

Charlie made a grimace and shook his head. "I told Ricky he would meet one of the most notorious men of our times tonight, and you sound like an old curmudgeon."

Eric laughed and drank some more champagne. "You shall have to look elsewhere, Ricky." He turned to Charlie. "I don't know why you would think of me. Notoriety has nothing to recommend itself. See where it left me?"

They both shook their heads and laughed at the irony of life.

"I have held something back from you," Charlie said. "I didn't want to ruin your day when we rode in the park and met Lenore."

Eric gave him a curious look. "What's that?"

"Mrs. Andrews is *née* Brigham. She is Cedric Brigham and Lord Denbury's sister."

"*What?*"

"I forgot about your involvement with Cedric, and she doesn't know you. However, I was surprised you didn't correct her when she started calling you Mr. Ramsey."

Eric stiffened with tension. "I didn't want her to recognize my name and run away in horror, but this is much worse. I remember that Cedric had a sister, but I never met her."

"She was away for years. Before she married, she spent time in the Colonies with some aunt or other. She's well past the bloom of her tender youth."

"Not *that* far." He eyed his friend and the wide-eyed Ricky. "If she discovers my real name, she'll faint dead away."

"Unlikely, but she'll treat you with icy politeness, or cut you outright."

Restlessness overcame Eric. "I shall take myself for a walk," he said. "At least no one can detect my notoriety in the dark."

"You have a point," Charles replied. "Anyway, Lenore has no need to know your identity. Just avoid further contact with her."

"You're right."

Eric put down his napkin, finished his claret, and went for a walk past the occupied boxes and out of the Grove. Agitation churned in his chest as all the memories of Cedric returned. He tried to push them back but was unsuccessful.

Chinese lanterns lit up the main walk, and he sauntered along, watching groups of strolling people and lovers with arms entwined. Many times he'd walked this path, and the other, darker paths. He had embraced many women, and stolen kisses from damsels behind trees, chaperones none the wiser.

He didn't mind that he didn't have anyone tonight, but it might get lonely in the long run. Kisses were not enough anymore. He longed to be truly close to someone.

A fountain trickled in the distance and it drew him closer. People stood in small clusters around it, and he noticed Mrs. Andrews's companions silhouetted against a lantern, deeply engrossed in a discussion. To his surprise he found Mrs. Andrews by herself, contemplating the sparkling water from a bench. Ludbank was nowhere in sight.

Acting on impulse, yet knowing he was playing with fire, Eric approached her. "The waterfall is quite striking against the lights, is it not?"

She looked up, startled. He sensed her pulling away even if she didn't move. "I daresay," she replied, not inviting further conversation.

"You look beautiful tonight," he said, meaning every word. His heart pounded in his chest.

Her keen gaze measured him for sincerity. "Thank you, but the exterior doesn't make the person."

"I realize that. And it never was truer. You would look beautiful in rags."

Her eyes filled with exasperation. "I should've known that you would invent some impossible reply."

"Why would you anticipate that?"

She shrugged. "I doubt that anyone could give you your comeuppance in conversation. I suspect you are an expert at glib evasions."

"I am a product of these elegant times. Conversation is an elegant art, don't you think?"

"I'm not going to get into a *conversation* about that." She looked toward the people coming down the walk. "My escort should be back shortly."

"Ludbank is at your beck and call tonight? Did you send him to fetch and carry?"

"I might see the humor in those remarks, but judging from the coldness of your voice, it seems you have little regard for the marquess."

"I don't know him very well, so I withhold my judgment."

"How grand of you," she retorted.

"As far as I know, he's an honorable fellow, but I never saw him in the role of lackey."

"Gentlemanly courtesy. Not that you would know what that entails."

"How can you berate me so without knowing me at all? I only engaged in this conversation to be polite. We have been introduced, and I anticipated acknowledging our acquaintance. As simple as that. Since you decided to get on your high horse, I realize my mistake."

She softened at that. "I didn't know what to expect. The evening has not gone well. I found out that Ludbank offends easily, and my unruly tongue put me in this position. Before I could make restoration, his coachman called him away on urgent business. He said he would return shortly, but I'm not convinced he will."

"That would not be the act of a true gentleman. He'll be back, but he should be here to protect you from the likes of me."

She laughed at that. "So he should, but I suspect he has a rather sharp temper and doesn't like to be gainsaid."

"What are you going to do if he doesn't return? If you were of inferior quality you would have a fit of the vapors."

"Truthfully, I've never succumbed to one, and I'm certain my friends will take me back home."

"Would you allow me?"

She eyed him curiously. "Why?"

He sought the right answer. "So that I know you arrive home safely."

"I have no fears of that, even if it means hailing a hackney."

"That would be unacceptable." He held out his arm. "Come. The night is young. Let us stroll down one of the walks until the marquess returns. I'm sure he will."

"Stroll in the dark so that you can take advantage of me?" A smile lurked at the corners of her mouth as she stood and placed her gloved hand in the crook of his elbow. They moved down the Grand Walk.

"I wouldn't mind, and you would not succumb to a fit of the vapors. In fact, I suspect you wouldn't reject an illicit tryst."

"Your opinion is more shocking than anything I've ever heard."

"But you don't flinch away."

"I'm not afraid of unwanted advances. I'm quite capable of defending myself."

"I'm sure you are. Do you carry a brick in that pearl-strewn reticule on your arm?"

"Always. I'm a vision of self-sufficiency."

"A vision you are, and I promise not to do anything to provoke your wrath."

"You are a most mysterious man."

"Not really, but I doubt that you would approve of me if you knew the whole story." Which she never would, he thought. He couldn't bear the thought of her fine eyes filling with disgust for the debacle of his past.

"How intriguing, a gentleman with a sullied reputation." She squeezed his elbow. "I'll soon find out everything. The gossipmongers never rest in this city."

"I don't picture you as someone who listens to salacious gossip."

"So it is salacious? That doesn't surprise me."

"All gossip is in a way. People feed on it like hungry dogs. It is not easy to be vilified, yet I don't care. Not anymore."

"Now I am more and more curious."

A couple greeted them on the path, and they nodded in return. The night had come alive with possibilities. He longed to kiss her, and sensed that under that cool exterior waited a passionate woman. Yet she guarded her inner self well, and he could understand that in view of her disappointment in marriage. As he walked beside her he felt like a cad for having read her diary in secret, though she fascinated him even more now that he had met her in person. If she ever found out the truth, she would be enraged, and it bothered him.

"I should like to know more about you," he said, as if he didn't already know quite a bit.

"My parents are gone. My brother Edward is the head of the family, and he is urging me to remarry, as I will then become one burden less."

"I don't see how you could ever become a burden, Mrs. Andrews. You mentioned your self-sufficiency earlier, and I don't doubt you on that."

"Thank you." She eyed him speculatively. "You differ from most gentlemen of my acquaintance, as you don't preach to me."

He recalled his acid comments in the diary, and knew her opinion would change drastically if she knew. Well, she would never find out. If she did, he would be long gone, as he planned to return to Swinmere in a couple of weeks. For now, he would enjoy the diversion of her company.

"I try to make the most of every moment. It's a waste of time to find fault with others as they will never change, no matter how much you preach."

She nodded. "True."

They walked across a gravel patch where repairs had

been made to the Walk, and she clung more tightly to his arm as her slippers struggled with the rougher surface. At one point, her hip touched his, and he steadied her. An urge to take her in his arms came over him, and he pulled her onto a narrow, unlit path.

"These places are made for lovers," he whispered as he swept her into his arms.

She protested, but he covered her mouth with his and savored the sweet taste of her. She whimpered, and then clung to his shoulders as if unable to stand on her own. Her warm response took his breath away, and for a moment he had the sensation of drowning.

He couldn't stop as he pressed her closer, and if she had complied he might have ravished her then and there among the dark trees. But she began to push against him, and he lifted his head, still dazed.

"Oh," she said, her lips still against his.

"Oh, yes," he replied and showered light kisses on her temple. "You are sweet nectar to my senses." He didn't want to let go. It had been so long since he had touched or been touched, and he realized the lack in his life.

She sighed against his lips, and he had to let go, hoping she wouldn't bolt, or fall into a diatribe. Her gaze burned him in the shadowy light filtering from the lanterns among the leaves. "I . . ." she began.

"Shh, do not talk. Words cannot describe the moment."

She didn't gainsay him, and he drew a breath of relief.

They stood in silence, staring at each other. Her shoulders looked tense, but her face had a soft expression, and she placed her hand over her heart. "It was unexpected," she whispered.

"Can we at least be friends? I know you have other plans for the future, and Ludbank has the tenacity of a terrier worrying a bone. He won't accept any kind of competition."

"You consider yourself competition?"

"Perhaps."

"Nonsense. It's too soon. Besides, I prefer my independence. No gentleman will bend me to his will." She flared her fan and started fanning her face as if too hot.

He felt hot as well, but gentlemen had to suffer with tight starched neck cloths and coats. He turned his face toward the slight breeze rustling in the trees. Without another word, he pulled her back onto the path and continued to walk. She didn't protest, for which he was grateful. Giggles came from another dark path, and he wondered if the suggestive sound mortified her, but she didn't seem to hear it.

Lenore walked as if asleep. His kiss had shaken her to the marrow, and she'd remembered the sweetness of Ronald's first kisses, and how elation had taken hold of her whole being. This was different. She didn't even know this man with whom she walked so carelessly in the dark.

"I think we should go back. Ludbank must wonder what happened to me." Was that faraway voice really hers?

"Yes . . . he will call me out if he sees you on my arm."

"Hardly. I would not let him," she scoffed. "He has no right to interfere in my life."

"He might not see it that way." He sighed heavily, and it raised a question mark in her mind.

"Why? You can't tantalize me with hints of scandal and not tell me the whole story. I'll perish with curiosity."

He looked at her quizzically. "This is not the right time and place, but I shall tell you the whole." He heaved another sigh. "You won't like it."

"Does it matter what I think?"

He didn't answer right away, but she sensed that it did matter. He carried a heavy burden, and it wouldn't be easy to share. This was only the second time she'd met him, and she hadn't liked him at all at their first encounter, but obviously she had fallen in with another gentleman with secrets. She shivered, recalling the horror of discovering that the love of her life had been so deceptive.

Never again. She would be excessively foolish if she repeated the mistakes of the past. Pulling away, she said, "I know I played a part in this, but please forget that it ever happened."

Chapter 4

Ludbank returned, looking for her at the fountain, and when he noticed her arrival with Mr. Ramsey on the Grand Walk, he stiffened noticeably. She wondered if he was going to make a scene, which made her uneasy. Expecting a confrontation, she was surprised to discover that Mr. Ramsey had disappeared, silent as a cat in the night. She was relieved, though her heart hammered with worry about the disconcerting situation.

"Who was that?" Ludbank demanded.

"Mr. Ramsey," she replied. "I took a walk and he accompanied me so that I didn't have to walk alone."

"Mr. Ramsey? Never heard of him." Ludbank's face was pale with suspicion.

"He's a friend of Sir Charles. I don't know him very well, but we've been introduced." That they certainly had been, she thought, remembering the sweetness of their kiss with a slight feeling of guilt.

Ludbank thought it over, and finally shrugged his shoulders. "Very well, I'm grateful he looked after you. It's not seemly for a lady alone to take walks in the dark. You should have asked Mrs. Montague to go with you." He gestured to the couple standing by the fountain. They had eyes for no one but themselves.

Ire rose in Lenore's chest. "I don't have to explain my actions to you, Malcolm. I'm quite capable of taking care of myself."

She could see the heat reddening his cheeks. His eyes smoldered, and she doubted that she would accompany him to any events again. She had no desire to deal with his anger. It didn't matter to her that he was a prime catch on the marriage mart. His courtship had flattered her, but was quickly turning into a burden.

"I see," he said.

"Pray don't make an issue of the situation. You left me here alone, and that's the end of it."

He puffed out his cheeks, but she ignored him and he swallowed the comment on his tongue.

"Please take me home."

Without another word, he gripped her elbow and steered toward the entrance to the Gardens.

Eric wandered along one of the paths, still dazed from his encounter with Lenore. Hers had been the sweetest lips he'd ever touched with his own. Could it be he'd never kissed the right mouth before? The thought that she might be the one woman who would truly matter disturbed him no end. Due to the circumstances, she was as unattainable as the stars.

She would never want him when she discovered his true identity. He had deliberately let her call him Mr. Ramsey, and the deceit would ruin everything between them. Not that there was much, yet everything. If he didn't acknowledge this yearning, this feeling of *rightness,* he would ultimately lose. Dear God, when had his life become so complicated?

He went in search of Sir Charles and found him with Ricky outside the Grotto, talking eagerly to a dragon of a lady with two young women and an older gentleman in tow. Eric recognized Miss Davina Bright, and he could understand Charlie's infatuation. Davina's smile sparkled and gleamed; she was yet another unattainable star. To Charlie she was indeed, but Eric knew his friend's adoration might be fleeting indeed.

Ricky sported a silly smile in the radiance of Davina's flawless beauty.

"If it's possible I'd like to extend an invitation to a picnic in the park this coming Thursday," Charlie said. "All of you, of course."

Perhaps he feared only the dragon would attend, Eric thought with a smile. He halted his approach and watched the exchange. The dragon didn't appear impressed, but Charlie didn't seem to notice. All he wanted was to feast his eyes on the fair Davina. Eric could understand him, but shallow beauty faded, and if there was little beneath the surface, they couldn't expect to build a deep relationship. He hoped that Charlie would see this if they spent any length of time together.

The dragon nodded, and then put her nose in the air and pulled the young woman with her. Ricky still held a silly smile on his face, and to Eric's surprise, Davina turned her head and gave him a smile over her shoulder. That was more than Charlie had received.

"Old fellow," Eric began as he joined his friend.

"Did you see her?" Charlie asked, his voice filled with longing.

Eric nodded. "She's a diamond of the first water. Are they coming to the picnic?"

"So you overheard. Yes, they are." Charlie clamped his hand on Eric's shoulder. "You're invited too."

"That might be a mistake. I know you are eager to include me as a friend, but I know you would regret it. Your goal is to collect favorable encounters with Miss Bright, not stave off possible scandal."

"Hmm. Where did you go anyway?" Charlie's gaze was still glued to the back of his beloved as she walked out of Vauxhall with her chaperone on one side, and the male protector on the other.

"I went to kiss a nymph."

Charlie laughed and Ricky looked impressed.

"Indeed," Charlie said. "Anyone I know?"

Eric didn't want to expose the truth. The revelation of Lenore's importance in his own life made it difficult to explain. He had not understood it himself, and he wondered if he ever could explain that elusive something she had inspired in him.

He wondered if she'd felt the same thing, and he suspected she had, but she might be too proud to admit it.

He would have to see her again soon.

Chapter 5

Rake every man over the coals and not expect resistance, she read in the diary and flung it on the bed next to her. The reply in the journal had not been as scathing as she had expected, as if the writer was tired, or lacking inspiration—or perhaps vitriol.

She pressed her fingertips over her eyes, willing away the headache pounding at her temples. The images of last night's event overcame her, and the memory of the tender kiss she'd shared with Mr. Ramsey made her feel even more miserable. How confusing life could be! She didn't even know his first name.

She moaned with frustration, and her maid, Mildred, came in with a basin of cold water laced with lavender oil and a towel to place on her mistress's aching head.

"Too much champagne I gather," she said, sniffing. Her face was a mask of disapproval. "'Tis not seemly to gallivant about town at all hours."

"Enough, Mildred. I won't hear a lecture from you. Not today."

"You received a letter this morning," Mildred said.

Lenore opened one eye and stared at the envelope. She opened it with little enthusiasm, her aching gaze focusing on Sir Charles's handwriting. He had invited her to a picnic on the morrow at Greenwich, a spur-of-the moment outing, he called it, and she decided it might be a good diversion to take her thoughts off the secretive Mr. Ramsey. She quelled her hidden desire to see him again and told herself not to hope that he might attend the picnic.

Groaning, she placed her hand over her eyes, and Mildred clucked her tongue.

"Headaches come from too much thinking," the maid said and placed the cold cloth over Lenore's forehead.

The cold soothed Lenore. "I shan't argue with you, but as far as I know, thoughts are never painful. They are phantoms."

"They cause pain!" the maid said with vehemence.

She might have a point, Lenore said to herself, because her thoughts about Mr. Ramsey surely had her agitated and he wasn't even in the room. "Sir Charles invited me to a picnic."

"These rustic entertainments will wear you down to the bone," the maid said with a sniff.

"It's the way of the world," Lenore replied with a sigh. She pressed the towel harder against her eyes and waved in the general direction of Mildred's voice. "Do go away, please."

Mildred let out another sniff and went to the door, her dress rustling. "Very well. There is no pleasing some people."

Lenore drifted off to sleep for half an hour, and when she awakened she felt much better. Her head had cleared, if not her thoughts, of the latest entry in the diary. The gall of the man, she thought as another wave of anger washed through her.

She ought to give him his comeuppance in public. Perhaps she would wait for him at the tearoom tomorrow. However, there was always the chance he would not appear. She flung off the knitted shawl covering her legs and went to her escritoire.

Opening her diary to a fresh page, she began to write.

At first you sounded as if you had some concern for me, but I soon realized that you are as insensitive as ever. And that you would be so sensitive as to put others' comforts before yours is ridiculous. I have never read so many untruths at once. If you had any sense of humor, you would not get into high dudgeon over my writings. I don't need lectures from the likes of you, and I don't need retaliation. If you had a single ounce of self-confidence, you would laugh at my tirades, but no, you have to write offensive replies, and that after you ruthlessly violated my privacy. That fact alone marks you as a cad—and callow. What I wrote about gentlemen to vent my frustration has hit its mark with you, and don't you dare gainsay me, as every word you've written attests to your arrogance.

You would not know the first thing about putting someone else's feelings before your own. I challenge you to prove me wrong, but since I don't know your identity, coward that you are, I cannot witness any gallantry on your part. I promise to look closely at every gentleman I meet to see if I can discover who you are. When I catch one looking down his nose most disagreeably, I shall know I'm in your presence.

She gave a delighted laugh at her daring. The man would be livid. Good! Feeling much better, she waited for the ink to dry, and then she closed the diary. She would send one of the servants to the Rose Tearoom with the journal. Before long the man would have it picked up and delivered to him. But the odd exchange was beginning to unsettle her, and once she received it back, she might burn the diary, get rid of it once and for all.

She went to the window and looked out at the street below. A servant walked a dog and an old woman hobbled along, swathed in a long gray cloak despite the warmth of the day. Lenore put her fingertips to her temple and rubbed. The memory of the kiss last night had awakened a longing for love, but she wondered if she would ever find someone who would not try to own her or belittle her in some way. Sighing, she touched her hand to her heart, knowing that at least she had peace if not love. The lonely yearning would recede with time.

She would surround herself with friends and dogs, and do without men forever.

The next morning she dressed in a white muslin gown with ruffles at the hem and around the neckline. A wide blue sash and a straw hat with a matching blue ribbon, gloves, and reticule completed the ensemble. Since the sun had dared to come out of hiding, she would bring a parasol to protect herself.

Charles would collect her in an hour, and she went downstairs to the dining room. The air smelled of coffee and bacon. She helped herself to a plate of bacon and toast. Beaton, the butler, served her steaming hot coffee.

"A lovely morning, ma'am," he said, his smile always at the ready. He had worked for Ronald twenty years, and Ronald had set great store by courtesy. Beaton's graciousness never faltered.

"Beaton, could I ask a great favor of you? I know you're wholly discreet, and that I can trust you."

He nodded and she asked him to return her diary to

the tearoom and wait to see who picked it up. Due to his servant's talent for seeming invisible, he would be the right person to garner information if there was any to be had. He bowed and complied. Perhaps she would know the identity of her correspondent before the day was over.

Sir Charles brought a young man in tow, his nephew Ricky.

"Charlie, why the hangdog expression?" she asked as she tied the hat ribbons under her chin.

"I had hopes to impress the fair Davina last night, but she paid me little heed."

"She smiled angelically at me," Ricky said gleefully and turned his entire body, as he couldn't turn his head due to extremely high shirt points. He wore a bright blue coat with exaggerated shoulders and a nipped-in waist, an exotic bird next to Charlie, in his coat of blue superfine and simple gray waistcoat.

Charlie's face fell even further. Evidently this piece of news was true, which affirmed Lenore's conviction that Davina was rather silly.

"Davina is famous for her smile," Lenore said and supplied one of her own. "Poets have written odes to her."

"I have not," Ricky said, raising his chin with pride.

"She smiles at everyone," Lenore said, trying to help Charlie forget these glum comments.

Charlie's lips drooped even lower. "She never smiles at me."

"You're wearing your heart on your sleeve, Charlie." She preceded them out into the sunshine and flared out her parasol. A footman placed her satchel in the boot of the coach. "Is anyone I know coming to the picnic, Charlie?"

He rattled off some names, but didn't mention Mr. Ramsey and her heart constricted. "Davina and her friends, and the chaperone Mrs. Millspoon will possibly attend, but I'm not sure. Mrs. Millspoon said last night that she doesn't want to tire her charge with too much activity. I pray they will be there."

"Ah! Now the truth comes out," Lenore said with a smile. "I knew I ought to bring my watercolors as everyone will be ignoring me and staring at the object of your affection."

The park at Greenwich was a haven of peace, enlivened by bird song. A light breeze ruffled the leaves and the grass. She breathed deeply of the fresh air and enjoyed the warmth of the sun on her back. The day was simply perfect. Squirrels rummaged in the grass for nuts, and a band of ducks flew overhead toward water. The bucolic idyll made her forget the annoyance of yesterday, and she was glad to discover that Belinda and Adam were invited too. Belinda had a stoic expression on her face, and Adam had already helped himself to a glass of hock from the table that had been set up under a wide-canopied oak.

Lenore saw plates of cross buns and scones, dishes of clotted cream, sweetmeats, bowls of fruit, plates of cold cuts, and bowls of nuts. She was sure the wine would flow freely, and she hoped that Adam wouldn't get into one of his moods and raise a ruckus.

Belinda smiled at her and kissed her on the cheek. "You look ravishing, Lenore."

"I do not. I have hollows under my eyes, owing to my sleepless nights."

"And why do you suffer through sleepless nights?"

Lenore shrugged. "Forgive me. I should not complain so. But the diary is still going back and forth, giving me bouts of wrath, and then there's Ludbank and his temper, not to mention—" She halted, as she was on the verge of telling Belinda about her night at Vauxhall Gardens. Her friend would not approve of a man who hadn't even told Lenore his first name. She excused herself. "I have something to ask Charlie, and then I'll be back."

She walked across the grass to the table where Charlie was busy instructing the servants, who had spread a pristine tablecloth on another table. "Charlie, please tell me, what is Mr. Ramsey's first name?"

Charlie stopped gesticulating as if his arms had suddenly locked in position. "What did you say?" His cheeks reddened as if embarrassed. "Mr. Rams—?"

"You know very well whom I mean."

"Eric," he said curtly. "Why do you want to know?"

"I saw him last night at Vauxhall."

Charlie nodded but was clearly uninterested in continuing the conversation. He turned his back in a nonchalant manner and addressed the servants anew. Lenore couldn't understand his abrupt behavior. She shrugged and moved on to speak with Belinda. Her friend sent an apprehensive glance toward her husband.

"He's already rather tipsy," she said. She pointed past her offensive husband at a group that had just arrived in a barouche. The ladies wore light-hued gowns and hats, creating a lovely picture against the greenery. "Look, there's the toast of the *ton*."

"Miss Bright?" Lenore shook her head in exasperation. "She's the sole reason we're here. Charlie is besotted with her, and Ricky is as well." She indicated the young man with a nod of her head. "His tongue is practically hanging out of his mouth, and that silly grin would make me run in the opposite direction."

Belinda laughed. "You are most unkind."

"Anyone can see that he— I daresay Charlie made a mistake bringing his nephew. You would think Charlie would have better judgment."

They noticed Davina's simpering smile as Ricky waved and made a deep bow. She hid her smile behind her fan and tilted her head sideways. "The minx," Lenore said, sotto voce. Charlie looked put out, to say the least, and belatedly saw his mistake in bringing Ricky to the picnic.

Charlie gave Lenore a lopsided smile as if he sensed her compassion. Yet she knew Davina was not the right woman for him. *How is it that we always fall in love with the wrong people?* she wondered. It was as if Cupid let loose his magical arrows in the dark.

"I brought my paints," Belinda said, "but Adam will complain if I stray too far from his side."

"He needs an audience," Lenore replied. She shaded her eyes with her hand. "He has one, so I don't know why we couldn't take a stroll before the food is served."

Belinda nodded, and they set off down a path through the woods, but as soon as they were out of sight, Adam called out to Belinda. She shrugged, her face a picture of resignation. "I shall have to go back."

"I will go on by myself then. Tell Charlie I shall return shortly."

"Don't stray too far. You are alone after all."

"Thank you, Belinda, but I am capable of taking care of myself."

She wandered along the sandy path, enjoying every step. Ronald had always wanted to live in the city, but Lenore had longings for a life close to nature. Her surroundings brought her back to her childhood and fond memories of her parents.

Ferns waved at the edge of the path, and she came to a large pond among the trees, where people were rowing a dinghy with leisurely strokes. She stood by the railing along the dock and gazed into the water. Sunlight illuminated tadpoles and small fish wiggling among the seaweed. To her surprise, she heard hoofbeats nearby on the path. She hadn't seen any riders, but the path curved around the pond and continued into the woods.

Was he following her? she thought as she recognized Eric Ramsey atop a tawny gelding. He halted on the grassy verge by the dock and lifted his hat in greeting.

"I didn't expect to see you here," she called to him and moved back toward shore.

He smiled and it transformed his serious face. "It is a pleasure to see you," he replied. "I thought it was a good day for a ride."

"Did Charlie invite you to the picnic?"

He didn't reply right away. "He hinted that he was going to Greenwich, and that he had invited friends for a picnic. He left the rest up to me."

She thought that a strange answer. Her heart hammered, and she knew she needed to stay away from him, or she might become embroiled in—she knew not what, precisely. There was danger in letting him into her life.

"I take it you were invited, Mrs. Andrews."

"Obviously." She wondered how best to disentangle herself from the situation. She resented the feelings he had stirred up.

He made as if to dismount. "Do you mind if I join you?"

"Yes, I do," she replied. "To put it bluntly, your company is unwelcome, Mr. Ramsey."

Chapter 6

"How can you be so cruel, Mrs. Andrews? After all, it is my birthday." Without waiting for another rejection from her, he stepped to the ground.

"Your birthday? I never knew." She blushed, as he stood next to her, so close she felt powerless to fight her attraction to him. The sensual gleam in his eyes compelled her to look away. "Happy birthday. I hope someone has planned a celebration for you."

"Not really. Charlie did, but he knows how I feel about gatherings."

"Nonsense. There are six people in our group, and you shall have to accept the company if anyone is to acknowledge your special day."

"There is no need to acknowledge it. I am a year older, that's all."

"Fiddlesticks. Why are you so stubborn? Everyone has the right to a celebration, however small. Charlie will be delighted to see you."

He seemed reluctant as he rolled the rim of his hat between his long fingers. "I . . . I don't want to put Charlie in an awkward position even if he invited me. You don't know—"

"Balderdash. You know as well as I that Charlie is the kindest and most generous of men." She pulled his arm, and he sighed as he grasped the reins and began leading the horse along the path.

"Are you——?"

"Am I . . . what?"

"Happy to see me."

She wished she could hide her blush, but it was more telling than any explanation, and she couldn't hope to lie and live with it. "Yes . . . and no," she said, her voice faint.

"A vexing reply. Can you explain?"

She squirmed under his scrutiny. It surprised her that he broke through her resistance with such ease. Though it seemed he could look through her and read what was hidden in her heart, he also seemed to be guarding his own. But why?

"I say yes because you intrigue me, mysterious man that you are, and no, because I have no desire to be involved in a romantic situation. I am at peace, alone at last, and grateful for it after the emotional storms I have lived through. I prefer to live quietly."

He pondered her reply in silence. "Thank you for being sincere," he said. "You have expressed sentiments that I share." He sighed and glanced ahead on the path. "Sometimes we do not have a choice, you know. Not everything is within our control."

She nodded. "I must and will control my life."

He chuckled and touched her arm with his hand. "I clearly hear Fate laughing at you."

"That is untrue," she retorted, riled.

"You *think* you are in control, but how many times has Fate tripped you? Be honest now."

She thought about it, knowing he was right, of course, but she could not admit that. "Must I explain myself to you? After all, this is only the third time we have met. I barely know you."

He nodded. "You're right. To be honest, I barely know myself."

She couldn't think of a proper reply. "Be that as it may. I must act according to my understanding."

"I believe your heart knows me."

The statement frightened her no end. He might be right and the truth stood right before her, tormenting her every breath. "I . . . don't want to discuss it. It is much too early for such talk."

"But I am your friend?"

She nodded. "I suppose, yet I'm reluctant to even call you friend as I know so little about you."

"I am not a talkative man. And if you knew the whole truth, you'd turn from me in disgust."

She smiled at him. "Oh? What atrocious crime have you committed? What is the secret you allude to every time I see you?"

He looked uncomfortable and pulled off one of his gloves to insert a finger between his neck and the starched collar. "'Tis hot today."

"Yes, summer is surely approaching."

They came around a copse of trees and she saw her friends standing and talking under the oak that sheltered the tables. "You should know you are among friends, Mr. Ramsey," she said.

Pain crossed his features, and he seemed reluctant to join the group, but she pulled him forward. The horse whickered softly, alerting the others. Charlie's face lit up. "Eric! You came after all. Happy birthday, old fellow."

Lenore couldn't understand the strange mood falling over the assembled guests. More of Charlie's friends, some unknown to her, had appeared in her absence. She noticed the pallor on Belinda's cheeks and the expression of dismay in her eyes. "Belinda, this is Charlie's friend, Mr. Ramsey."

Belinda shook her head as a murmur rose among the others present. "No, Lenore, you are mistaken. This is Mr. Eric Ramsdell, the man who's said to be responsible for your brother's death."

As if a boulder had fallen on her head, Lenore staggered sideways, struggling to catch her breath. A wave of utter weariness weighed her down. Everything seemed to slow down, the guests speaking soundlessly, and the scene before her started spinning. For the first time ever she felt faint, but resisted as she clung to Belinda's proffered arm.

Eric's face had lost all color, and he backed away, pulling his horse with him as he still held the reins. "I should take my leave."

Everyone watched in tense silence.

"You were introduced as Mr. Ramsey," Lenore said, her mouth paper dry. She swallowed hard.

Eric shook his head. "You assumed my name was Ramsey."

"You never corrected me, and now I know why."

"Would you have ever considered talking to me if you knew my true name?"

She shook her head, and the world started spinning again. Someone offered her a chair to sit on, and she sank onto it, her legs like jelly. "You deceived me," she said, filled with disappointment. "Why I would ever trust you?"

"I didn't—"

"Don't even try to defend yourself," she spat, and the onlookers murmured their approval—all except

Charlie, who went to Eric and placed a hand on his arm. Eric pried it away gently.

"Old friend, return to your guests, or you'll end up a pariah too."

Charlie obeyed, his eyes filled with misery.

"Why would you take his side, Charlie?" someone asked harshly. "Though not convicted, he's a murderer."

Charlie spread out his hands in bewilderment. "Nothing was ever proven. Eric cannot be a murderer. I've known him for a very long time."

No one replied. The icy silence was enough to condemn a whole slew of criminals. The happy mood had disappeared, and Lenore could only struggle with her disappointment, knowing it would never go away.

"I declare, you people," Charlie said with a huff.

"Why did you introduce us, Charlie?" Lenore asked.

"I forgot the connection with your brother momentarily, and you were painting in the park. I couldn't very well ignore you."

Eric had removed himself from the picnic area, and swung himself into the saddle. Without a backward glance, he urged his horse into a canter.

"I'm appalled that he would try to worm his way into your life under a false name, Lenore. He must have known your identity," Belinda said.

"I'm sure he did, but a man like that will stop at nothing to gain his objective. I would say he is wholly unscrupulous." Lenore sighed and fought back her tears.

"Lenore," Charlie pleaded, "I doubted you would meet again. I had no intention to bring you back together after that first time in the park."

The picnic had lost the air of gaiety that had preceded Mr. Ramsdell's appearance. The mood remained
subdued, and when it started raining an hour later, the
servants packed up the picnic paraphernalia and the
guests took refuge in their carriages.

Lenore just wanted to leave, and Charlie looked as
if he'd lost everything. The fair Davina had left earlier
without a look in his direction. Mrs. Millspoon said
she'd never been so offended as when Eric appeared
and that she would never attend another gathering that
Charlie hosted. Davina had only kept her nose in the
air. She had once again smiled at Ricky, who might be
the only one in the party wearing a grin on his face.

Chapter 7

Eric suffered the torment of someone waiting for his execution. One of the footmen had retrieved the diary from the Rose Tearoom, and Eric held it between the palms of his hands. The deception was weighing heavily on him, and he knew that he should have told Lenore his real name and let the whole truth be known. He'd sensed she would not approve of the subterfuge, and he had tried to gain time with her. The delight of her presence had clouded his better judgment, and now he had to suffer for it. Who would have thought she was Cedric Brigham's sister?

The journal seemed to burn him and he let it drop onto his desk. He had never considered himself a coward, but surely he had acted like one, and the business with the diary had been most underhanded. What had begun as a lark, a diversion, had quickly turned into something he cared deeply about. Lenore deserved better than the scolding words he'd written in her diary, only for the thrill of sparring with her.

She had scolded him back, but he deserved it.

He sighed and wondered if his life would be forever marked by the shattering event of Cedric's death. Either he could choose to act like a victim, or he could make more inquiries into the past. Someone had killed Cedric. He had not, even though every finger pointed at him.

He got up from the wing chair in his grandfather's library and started pacing, studying the intricate pattern of the red-gold Oriental carpet but not really seeing it. His ostracizing at the picnic had jolted him from apathy. It was about time he cleared his name. There had to be a way to find out the truth even if he hadn't succeeded before.

Sir Winton Niles had been at one of the posting inns along the way to Brighton, and Eric knew he had been Cedric's worst enemy. But how could he prove that Sir Winton had been the one who fired the shot that killed Cedric? He had an alibi and a witness who claimed he had stayed at the posting inn, yet Eric could have sworn he'd seen Sir Winton ride off just before he and Cedric continued the phaeton race.

Something had felt wrong; he'd had a premonition of disaster to come. In fact, Eric had experienced an overwhelming desire to call off the race, despite the possibility of being named a coward. He wished he had heeded his inner voice; he would still have an unsullied reputation and Cedric would still be alive.

He wished he could confide in someone. He had expressed his concerns to his grandfather when the shooting took place; and, filled with gratitude, he'd witnessed his grandfather step in and demand a thorough investigation when they wanted to throw the blame on Eric.

No evidence of any sort had come to light.

Some said Cedric had committed suicide, making a flamboyant spectacle of himself; others said Eric had shot him to make sure he didn't win the race. But he'd had no motive. He certainly didn't need the thousand pounds that the bet entailed.

He would have to make another effort to find the woman, Minette Sharp, who had given Sir Winton an alibi at the time of Cedric's demise. He'd walked down that road where Cedric died a number of times, but perhaps he'd missed something. This time he had to prove his innocence, or forever live a shadow life at Swinmere.

Lenore had inspired this newfound courage. But unless he could clear his name, he would never stand a chance with her.

He looked at the diary again and read the passages he'd written. Her last scathing reply had brought him an understanding of her strength. She would never give in to him unless she chose to.

Perhaps if he could explain himself better, get her to see his true character . . . Once she found out his real identity, she would be furious.

With a heavy sigh, he opened the diary on his desk and sat down to compose a message.

Perhaps I'm not what you think—and I know that I harbor no resentment toward you despite your harsh words, which for the most part are true.

I intend to prove to you that I care about people's—your—feelings, as I claimed in an earlier entry. And I hope you will confide freely in me. Not all gentlemen are cads, and we are certainly capable of listening if we put our minds to it. If truth be known, gentlemen want and need intimacy and understanding, just as women do.

That is a very simple fact, and if we can agree on that much, we shall gain something from this exchange. You may want to know who I am, but for now, it is better that you do not.

Eric put the quill down and spread some sand on the pages.

His reply was straightforward enough. He had not written a single prickly statement and he was proud of himself. Perhaps he could smooth over the roughness of the previous entries, but knew all too well that Lenore would never forgive him if she found out who her correspondent really was. He would see to it that she never would, or all his efforts would be for naught.

In a foul mood, Lenore went downstairs the next morning after a sleepless night. When Eric Ramsdell's true identity had been revealed, she had been furious, and the emotion had lingered long into the night. Pure exhaustion had finally consumed her, but she had only enjoyed two or three hours' sleep at best. She addressed Beaton, the butler, in the dining room. "Did you discover who retrieved my journal at the Rose Tearoom yesterday?"

"I am afraid it was a servant. The staff didn't know him, and he was too quick for me outside. I never caught up with him, but I know what he looks like—a tall, brawny fellow. The next time, I shall catch him and make him tell me who his master is." Beaton straightened his back for emphasis. "Just give me some more time, Mrs. Andrews, and the answer shall be yours."

"Very well," she said with a sigh. "Thank you, Beaton." She would have to remain patient for a while longer. "You might as well spend the morning at the Rose Tearoom and retrieve the diary when he returns."

"Perhaps it's a servant at the establishment who . . . ?" Beaton's eyes grew round at the thought of such insolence.

She shook her head. "No, the unknown gentleman who corresponds with me is educated."

Beaton looked relieved. "Very good, ma'am. Just the idea of some commoner making himself familiar with you—"

Lenore wagged her finger. "You are a snob, Beaton."

"Hmph." He cleared his throat. "'Tis rather an *unusual* circumstance, if you don't mind me saying so," he said.

"You are entitled to your opinions, Beaton. Our correspondence is a diversion, something out of the ordinary, and surely no harm will come out of it."

"Highly irregular," he said with a sniff.

She laughed, but not from joy. "You sound very much like Mildred. I'd prefer that you keep the gossip to a minimum."

He nodded, puffing out his chest. "Ma'am, I never engage in gossip."

"That's a plumper if I ever heard one. Everyone does, including myself."

He looked none too pleased and went in search of the coffeepot to serve her a cup before he went to look for the diary.

To her surprise, she'd barely finished her breakfast before he returned. "It had already been delivered, ma'am, just as they opened. I never had the chance to apprehend the servant."

She received the leather-bound journal. "Very well. Thank you, Beaton."

Taking the book with her, she went to the front parlor, where sunlight was streaming through the window. With a cup of coffee at her elbow, she began reading, scanning the lines for slurs and insults. There were none! "Oho," she exclaimed out loud. "Now he wants to be my confidant. And hopes I will share my feelings with him. The power it would give him!" She laughed at the obvious ploy. "This man is clever." If she wrote about her latest fiasco, he would probably find a way to publish it and make a profit.

In a fit of anger, she ran upstairs and sat down at her desk. Gripping her quill hard and dipping it in ink, she wrote:

> *Of all the impertinent suggestions! Do you consider me lacking in intelligence? Your proposal is preposterous. I suggest you find something else to occupy your mind, as this is the last time I shall write a response to you. This has gone on long enough, and my patience is at an end.*
>
> *My mind is made up about you—I shall never trust you. To divulge my innermost heart to a gentleman who has professed a lowly opinion of females is out of the question. I would only set myself up to ridicule.*
>
> *I entreat you—no, I demand that you accept this as the end of our conversation!*

Content, she signed her name and blotted the ink. This should teach him! Going in search of more coffee in the dining room, she hoped that Beaton could waylay the servant on the morrow and find some answers. Mayhap she could give her secret critic pause, discover a way to touch his most vulnerable spots with some pointed criticisms of her own.

This man made her temper rise every time she saw his forceful handwriting. When she discovered his identity, she would give him a rakedown that would make all others pale by comparison.

"Gentlemen have given me nothing but heartache," she said to the room.

Silence reigned, and dust motes danced in the bright light. A morning ride might be just the thing to dissolve her exasperation. She went to change, and heard a commotion at the door. Her brother, the Earl of Denbury, stood on the threshold while Beaton smiled with happiness to see him. All the servants adored her older brother.

"Edward, what a surprise," she said with little enthusiasm. Not that she disliked her brother, but she knew why he was here. "It's good to see you abroad on a lovely morning like this."

"Yes, sister dear," he said, his voice heavy. He handed his beaver hat and gloves to Beaton.

"I'm about to ride. Will you join me?"

"I came in my carriage. I'm on my way to the club to meet an old friend. Perhaps some other day."

She scrutinized her tall brother. He looked as elegant as ever in a coat of blue superfine, yellow pantaloons, and Hessians polished to a high luster. His hair had been arranged in curls and the gold fobs and chains over his flat middle gleamed as if newly polished. But there were dark circles under his eyes, as if he still didn't sleep much. He had never gotten over Cedric's death, she knew.

"Come into the dining room," she said. "The morning coffee is still hot, and it will do you good."

He nodded gratefully, and followed her there. She added sugar and milk to the coffee, just the way he liked it. They sat together on a pair of chintz-covered chairs by the open window. Gold-fringed green curtains waved in the gentle breeze, and birdsong reached their ears.

"You don't look happy," she said, and braced herself. "I heard rumors, and I had to find out for myself if they are true. You went with Sir Charles Minion to a picnic and you walked and conversed with Mr. Eric Ramsdell, the man who killed our brother. That kind of gossip made my blood run cold, as you might understand, dear sister."

"Yes . . . I can see your point. The rumors are true. But I did not intend to speak with Mr. Ramsdell—in fact, I had no idea about his identity until someone informed me."

"It's also said you've spoken with him on previous occasions."

Anger edged her reply. "Who is spying on me?"

"No one in particular. You have to remember I know a great many people in London, and you've been seen in public places with this infamous fellow. How he can show his face in London after what happened, and presume to speak to you, is beyond me."

"He might not have known my connection to Cedric, and if he did, he would have known any conversation would go nowhere." She thought of their kiss at Vauxhall Gardens and cringed with guilt.

"Of course he knew about your connection," Edward said coldly. "The man is trying to push his way back into our lives, and I shan't have it. He's only here to torment us." He gave her a stern glance from under his dark eyebrows. "You've been bold as brass, Lenore, and I am most displeased. I hear you're giving Ludbank a difficult time as well. Why must you provoke him? If you marry him, you'll be fixed for life."

"But I don't love Ludbank. The only reason I've spent time with him is because he's so persistent. I have no idea what he sees in me, and truthfully, I don't see a future with him." She knew that would annoy her brother, but she had to make him realize what her intentions were.

"Indeed. Any unwed female would be delighted to have his attention, but you turn up your nose and only find fault with the poor fellow. He's approached me with the objective of gaining my permission to court you. He wants to ask for your hand in marriage."

"He is not the man for me, and he ought to see that. He's wasting his time, which I've told him in no uncertain terms."

"Thunder and turf, have you completely lost your mind?" Now the anger was evident in the high color of Edward's face. "I want to see you married and settled by the end of the year."

"'Tis a dream of yours, maybe, but not mine. We have to differ, and you have no command over my life anymore."

He hit the armrest of his chair with his fist. "But I worry about you, Lenore."

"I don't, so why would you?" She was getting more and more annoyed with the conversation. As a widow she had at least a modicum of freedom, and this town house and the money Ronald had left her. She had few worries in the world.

"You cannot simply do as you please!"

"What do you mean, Edward?"

"I demand that you bring a chaperone everywhere you go, and always keep a companion. It is unseemly for you to live here all by yourself. I shall ask Aunt Rose to move in with you."

"I won't have any of our spinster aunts here, and that's the end of it! Each one is fussier than the next, and I won't tolerate them putting their noses into my life." She rose and held out her hand toward her brother. "You know I love you. We must not quarrel like this."

He heaved a sigh filled with foreboding. "You are far too strong-willed for your own good," he replied, but he obeyed. He looked down at her, as he made ready to leave. "I will have to keep an eye on you from a distance, but never forget that I'm watching."

"What you must do is get over Cedric's death, Edward. How will you ever find a wife if you keep moping around that mausoleum of yours in Grosvenor Square?"

"All in due time," he snapped. "Mind your own business, and make sure you live above reproach or there will be repercussions. I won't have the family name dragged through the mud because you see fit to hobnob with all and sundry—with cold-hearted *murderers*."

Lenore turned hard inside. "You are exaggerating, Edward. I did not deliberately go out of my way to speak with Mr. Ramsdell, and I assure you, there will be no more contact."

He sighed, his back ramrod straight. "See to it that there isn't. I won't tolerate it, and I'll find a way to banish you from London."

Lenore's patience snapped, and she could have shouted her anger from the treetops, but she kept her silence as she walked in front of him to the door. "I daresay you believe I'm so immature that I need supervision."

"You must govern yourself, sister." Edward thanked her for the coffee and took his hat and gloves from Beaton. He turned anew to Lenore. "Have I made myself clear? If you don't want Aunt Rose bearing down on you, behave accordingly."

She nodded mutely, stiff with anger inside. As soon as he left, she dressed in a riding habit of blue velvet with gold-plaited trim and ordered to have her horse brought around from the mews. Beaton inquired as to whether she wanted a groom to accompany her, but she said no.

Her mixed emotions locked inside, she didn't know where to go or how to release them. Perhaps Belinda could help her sort through the confusion.

She missed Cedric. With time, she'd accepted his death, but the realization she'd kissed his killer made her cringe with guilt. She'd never wanted to sully Cedric's memory, but that was exactly what she had done.

It seemed everyone was staring at her as she rode across Mayfair to Berkely Street, where the Chandlers lived. Belinda was at home, dressed in a frilly white dressing gown and a huge lace-edged mobcap. She was sipping chocolate and eating a slice of toast in her bedroom. Spread before her on the table was the latest issue of *La Belle Assemblée.* "The dresses are becoming fuller," she said as a greeting.

"We'll have to consult our modistes," Lenore said without enthusiasm.

"I knew you would come here," Belinda said, her gaze searching Lenore's. "You're my friend, and I'm glad of it," she added.

Lenore started crying at those simple words. "Life could be so much easier if everyone were friends." She dabbed at her eyes and her nose with a handkerchief she'd pulled out of her pocket.

Belinda smiled, and sipped her chocolate. "Your freedom has irked a lot of people," she said. "And now your actions have gone beyond the pale."

"Edward threatened to bring in one of the spinster

aunts, or pack me off to the country. He doesn't know the worst, or I would surely be gone already."

"The worst?" Belinda set down her cup, and a frown line deepened between her eyebrows.

"You met Mr. Ramsdell yesterday, Belinda. But I have met him before, and I actually shared a kiss with him that brought down the heavens."

Belinda gasped. "When?"

"At Vauxhall. Ludbank was called to deal with a problem and I went for a walk with Mr. Ramsdell—or Ramsey, as I thought before I knew his real identity."

Belinda's eyes grew larger. "He took advantage of you?"

"Yes. I let him." Lenore sighed and sank down at the opposite side of the table. "How can I ever live with myself again?"

"Lenore, you were deceived and Ramsdell took advantage of you. He must have known who you were, and still he pursued."

"Yes, I don't doubt it. Charlie certainly knew, and I won't talk to him again unless he can explain his conduct."

"His position is precarious at best. Do not judge him too harshly as his loyalties are divided. He cannot choose sides."

"He has chosen. He took Ramsdell's side by not confiding the truth to me. And he introduced us!"

"Perhaps he forgot about the past."

"That's what he said." Lenore thought about his strange change in behavior at Green Park when she'd mentioned her brother's death. "Charlie is forgetful at best." She glanced at her friend. "You are very astute. Charlie is fortunate to call you his friend. I was ready to skin him alive."

Belinda laughed. "Charlie is a bumbling cloth head, but I've always liked him. He is kind through and through."

Lenore agreed. He would never willfully hurt her. "Well, then—I feel better. I am grateful that I don't have to lose Charlie."

"I'm certain he will be properly apologetic." Belinda smoothed the crumbs off her dressing gown.

"All of this brought back the horrors I'd put behind me, or so I thought."

"'Tis difficult to say who hated Cedric enough to kill him. It would take a ruthless man, and I'd say Mr. Ramsdell has hidden depths. Who knows what grudge he harbored against your brother?"

"Cedric was headstrong and arrogant. It's possible he taunted the killer, just for the thrill of teasing Fate."

"He was rather a hothead."

"But he had a kind side, and he loved children. 'Tis a pity he never had the chance to raise his own. The murderer took that away from him."

"I doubt Cedric ever really grew up. Children sensed that in him."

Lenore smiled. "Your observation is astute. His life was short, but a very happy one."

"*You* need not suffer any longer, Lenore."

Lenore sighed and rubbed her temples. A headache had started and she asked for a cup of tea to soothe her pain. Belinda called her abigail from the adjoining room and asked her to fetch the tea. Tears gathered in Lenore's eyes.

"I don't know if the killer was punished enough, Belinda."

"He's an outcast in London, and always will be. Even though they couldn't prove he was guilty, it doesn't matter. The judgment might as well be branded on his forehead."

"If he shot Cedric as everyone suspects, he's a cold and evil man to walk around London as if nothing happened. He doesn't honor life."

"You would do well to stay away from him, or you might fly into a rage and do him an injury," Belinda said, her face serious. "If only we could prove his guilt."

Lenore straightened her back and wiped away her tears with the back of her hand. "What if I could?"

"How would you do that? The Bow Street runners found no weapon or any other evidence, and no witnesses were present on that lonely stretch of road. If it hadn't been for the violent quarrel Cedric had with Mr. Ramsdell at the posting inn where they changed horses, they had no motive to pin on him. It is a fact that Ramsdell was right behind Cedric on the road."

"Then I shall prove him guilty if it's the last thing I do."

Chapter 8

Lenore felt better after her conversation with Belinda. Despite her own rather desperate marital situation, her friend always had an ear to lend and good advice to give. Lenore decided to ride across Berkely Square to enjoy the breeze before she returned home to plot her strategy to prove Mr. Ramsdell's guilt.

People had begun to return to their country estates. The Season was coming to an end, and Lenore longed to breathe the fresh air of the country. She would spend some weeks with Belinda at the Chandler estate, but not before she had a chance to investigate Cedric's death. She would start by contacting the Bow Street runner who had been in charge of the investigation.

Her horse turned the corner of the street at a quick pace. A newssheet blew ahead of the mare, bouncing against the cobbles, and flapping like a bird as the wind rose between the houses. Her mount started sideways and almost collided with another rider as he rode around a farmhand pushing a wheelbarrow full of potatoes.

His horse brushed against her leg, almost knocking her to the ground. She clung desperately to the sidesaddle but lost her balance as her mare shied away from the other horse. As Lenore slid to the ground, she glanced at the rider, a reproof on her tongue. Her breath caught as she recognized Eric Ramsdell, and her foot hit the uneven surface of a cobblestone. Her ankle twisted and she fell, crying out with pain.

"Mrs. Andrews! Are you hurt?"

She noticed the concern in his voice as he bent down on one knee beside her. He took her arms, but she pushed him away. "Stay away from me!"

"Are you hurt?" His grip hardened around her arms, and he pulled her upright even as the horses stamped nervously beside them. She noticed vaguely that onlookers took charge of the mounts. As she pushed her weight onto the injured ankle, pain flared up immediately. *I must have sprained it,* she thought, cursing herself under her breath.

"Please leave me alone."

"I'll take you home."

"You shan't. Stay away from me."

His eyes looked wounded, and the dark circles under them betrayed his sleepless nights. He still held tight around her arms, and she couldn't find the strength to pull away. She glanced at the onlookers, desperately looking for someone who could release her from Mr. Ramsdell and assist her into the saddle. As long as she got home, someone could help her there.

"You cannot refuse," he insisted. "It is the least I can do. I would not leave you exposed here all by yourself."

Her head started spinning. This was her worst nightmare, and she was trapped. Tears welled into her eyes, partly due to the pain, partly due to her frustration. "Do not touch me," she said, her voice hoarse with emotion.

"Nonsense! You can't remain here in the dust." He held her by the waist and called to one of the onlookers to bring the mare around. The man obeyed, and Eric lifted Lenore into the saddle. Her ankle twinged with pain, and she brushed hot tears from her cheeks. Never had she been more mortified. Unwilling to create a scene in public, she had to play her role and escape as soon as they were left alone.

"I'm going to take you to Berkely Square and deliver you into my grandmother's care."

"No, absolutely not!" she said between gritted teeth, but he'd taken the mare's reins and led both horses toward the square, which was only steps away. He must have just left from there. She hadn't known he lived at Berkely Square. How could this have happened? Her emotions in turmoil, she clung to the saddle. Without control of the reins, she couldn't escape. Drat the man!

"Here we are," he said as they stopped before an imposing stone mansion with Grecian columns holding up the roof over the front entrance. A wide staircase led to two oak doors inlaid with stained-glass. Urns holding some kind of yellow flower flanked the door. Above the lintel hung a red-and-white crest depicting two crossed arrows and a running deer in one corner and a fleur-de-lis in the other.

Eric opened the door and a tall, slim butler appeared, his expression turning to confusion as he watched Lenore on the horse.

"Lawrence, this is Mrs. Andrews. She has had an accident, and I want two of the footmen to carry her into the parlor. Also, please inform Lady Blythe."

"Very good, sir." Lawrence bowed and spoke with two footmen hovering in the background.

Before a cat could blink, Lenore found herself seated, legs up, on a chaise longue in the front parlor, which was decorated in soft greens and grays. A

gold-bordered green carpet enlivened the otherwise oppressively dark furniture. The clutter of
carved boxes, brass candlesnuffers, doilies, tiny
porcelain vases, and figurines closed in on Lenore,
but she admired some of the tall silver candlehold-
ers on the table before her. A few seconds passed
and she had barely composed herself when a regal
lady dressed in puce bombazine sailed into the
room.

"Good morning, Mrs. Andrews," she said with great
politeness. Her blue eyes held a certain hauteur, but
Lenore sensed a great deal of kindness. "I am Lady
Blythe, Mr. Ramsdell's grandmother."

Lenore nodded. "Good morning." She looked for
Eric, but he had not accompanied Lady Blythe into
the room.

"I heard you had an accident." She sat down on a
chair nearby. "Eric is sending for the doctor. We must
make sure you are not seriously injured before we
take you home."

"That is most kind of you, Lady Blythe, but wholly
unnecessary. Please just convey me home, where I can
recover. This is a minor inconvenience. All I need is
to rest."

"We must make sure nothing is broken. The con-
sultation will be brief. You must be in great pain."

"I feel a dull ache, but I am certain it's only a sprain."

"Nevertheless, we shall make sure. Eric feels responsible for you. He told me how you and he almost
collided." She reached toward Lenore's feet. "You
could have had a serious injury. Let me help you with
your half boot before the swelling gets too great to
remove it." She began unlacing Lenore's boot.

"Did he also tell you who I really am?"

"I know of you, as I know others of the *ton* without really being acquainted." The older woman shook her head as she gently pulled the boot off the swelling foot. Lenore winced with pain.

"I am Cedric Brigham's older sister, Lenore."

The older woman dropped the boot on the floor with a thud. Her mouth dropped and her chins wobbled as she swallowed. "I am speechless."

"And here I sit in my enemy's lair," Lenore held up her hand, "not that I have any quarrel with you, pray forgive me, Lady Blythe, but I realize Mr. Ramsdell lives with you."

"Mrs. Andrews. I had no idea." The old lady smoothed the skirt of her gown nervously, and then she straightened, giving Lenore an imposing look. "I'll have you know that Mr. Ramsdell is no murderer. Though I wasn't there when poor Mr. Brigham died, I assure you that Eric did not pull the trigger of that pistol. It's not in him. Even hunting never caught his interest, and I never saw him have more than the most cursory interest in weapons. Like most gentlemen he likes the pugilist society and gaming, and even books. He has an artistic eye, and has painted many of the pictures that hang here."

She pointed at one, a portrait of a horse and its owner, displayed over the marble fireplace. "That is my husband at Swinmere with his favorite horse, Springer."

Lenore viewed the fair rendering and knew that Eric had many talents. "Yes, I can see his gift, but he's also very good at turning words to his advantage."

"When he was younger, yes, he always had a glib explanation for everything. Whatever plan he was pursuing, he managed to convince someone of the brilliance of his plan. He never failed to succeed." She sighed. "Although some plans were not the most well-laid. But he has changed completely. He is more considerate; he weighs the validity of other people's opinions. In other words, he has matured."

"*Someone* killed my brother, and the only man present was your grandson."

"As far as we know. Eric turned the world upside down to find some answers, but never did. He had to finally retreat to Swinmere to avoid the vicious gossip of his enemies."

"He is guilty unless he can prove otherwise in my eyes—even if the law conveniently lets the matter pass. The future Lord Blythe is certainly much more powerful than the second son of an earl. Whatever Cedric had, he gambled away."

"Yes, they were two peas in a pod. I had a liking for Cedric, always happy, always with a ready compliment on his tongue. Rather a charmer, I'd say."

"He had the kindest heart."

"And a recklessness that matched Eric's. It could have been Eric who died that day. They were carefree, living one day at a time. How immature and reckless, but that's how they were."

"My other brother, Lord Denbury, has never gotten over Cedric's death. I believe he considers himself responsible in a sense. He abhorred Cedric's reckless behavior."

"Yes . . . I do understand that sentiment, but Cedric would always do what he wanted. He was always ready for some mad lark. A gathering that had Eric and Cedric on the guest list was never boring."

Lenore smiled. "You have a point. Cedric's cheerful manner always lifted everyone out of the doldrums."

Lady Blythe rang a silver bell on the table and the butler entered. "Bring us a tea tray, Lawrence." He bowed and left without a word.

Lady Blythe offered her some chocolate bonbons from a crystal bowl. Despite her reluctance to take anything from Mr. Ramsdell's family, she picked one, and found a creamy center as she bit into it. The chocolate melted in her mouth. She found herself liking the old lady, yet this was a most awkward situation.

"I don't go out in society much these days, or I would have met you," Lady Blythe said and popped a bonbon in her mouth.

Lenore nodded. "I'm sure. However, I'm tired of the balls and routs. It is a relief that the Season is mostly over."

"Hmm, everything is much too extravagant these days. I have no patience with it all. I am only invited to card parties, and that is enough for me."

"Another clever card player in the family?" Lenore said with a laugh. She almost swallowed her tongue, not believing she dared to tease a lady she had only just met.

Lady Blythe's lips twitched. "Eric learned all his card tricks from me," she said with a chuckle.

At least she had a sense of humor, Lenore thought. "You must have been a good teacher. He took such a liking to gaming."

"He has a keen mind and a good memory. As a boy he had an insatiable thirst for knowledge." She sighed. "The boy was often lonely. His parents died young and he had no brother or sister. We did our best, my husband and I, but it's never the same. Every child needs his parents."

"Yes . . . I agree, but Eric lacked for nothing under

your wing. His subsequent conduct flew in the face of what you taught him."

Lady Blythe did not reply, and she dropped the subject as the tea tray arrived on the arms of a lackey wearing a blue satin coat and a powdered wig. He set it down and left.

"Please have some tea to soothe your nerves," the lady said and poured two cups. She gave Lenore hers, and after she had taken two sips, the door opened again. This time Mr. Ramsdell entered with a short, rotund man who was undoubtedly the doctor.

"Dr. Bradon, this is Mrs. Andrews," Lady Blythe said.

The doctor bowed as much as his paunch allowed. "I hear you had an accident, my dear," he said and studied her bare ankle through his eyeglass.

Lenore sensed Mr. Ramsdell's eyes on her, but she refused to acknowledge him, yet was highly aware of her own reaction as her heart raced and her cheeks turned hot. Her enemy should not have the power to affect her heart, she thought, angry at the betrayal of her body.

Lady Blythe said, "Eric, it's not seemly . . . your presence . . ."

She didn't have to say another word. He left, closing the door softly behind him. Lenore sighed with relief, and Lady Blythe gave her a probing stare. She wanted to hide her blushing face, but couldn't.

The doctor lifted the hem of Lenore's dress no more than an inch and prodded her ankle. He hummed to himself and sighed several times. She moaned when he gently twisted the ankle to one side.

"Not broken, but sprained. There will be a nasty bruise on your foot for some time. Rest with the leg elevated and cover it with cold compresses, and this will heal rather quickly." He glanced at Lady Blythe. "If she remains here, make sure she follows my orders."

"Oh, no," Lenore hastened to say. "I live on Albemarle Street, but I assure you I'll follow your recommendations."

"But you are welcome to stay here for a few days," the older lady said. "I would enjoy your company."

"Thank you, but you have been very gracious already. I could not impose on you any longer."

"Fiddlesticks. It is not an imposition." She stood, thanking the doctor. "Send Mr. Ramsdell the bill," she said before Lenore could protest. "My grandson was at fault here. He was very clumsy, which is unusual for him."

The doctor bowed once more and left.

"I shall have Eric escort you back home. That's the least he can do."

"I'd rather not," Lenore said, alarmed.

"Nonsense, he owes you that much, and I wouldn't send you out with just the servants. You shall ride in my coach, and one of the grooms can bring your horse back."

Lenore saw the pugnacious thrust of Lady Blythe's chin and decided that she had no choice. It pained her no end. She sat up and placed her foot on the floor, and as the blood went back down, a wave of excruciating pain traveled with it. She closed her eyes for a moment to stem the agony.

Lady Blythe helped her put her white stocking back on. The foot had swelled even more. Before long it would be in the shape of a ball, she thought. This was the last thing she needed.

She braced herself as Lady Blythe called her grandson.

Evidently he'd been waiting outside. He came in, carrying Lenore's riding gloves and crop.

"I shall escort you home," he said before Lady Blythe could speak.

"I told Lady Blythe that it's not necessary." Her voice petered out.

He didn't listen. Lenore wanted to cry when he picked her up in his arms as easily as if she were a feather and carried her outside. His arms felt safe and strong, but she lay stiff and awkward against him, trying to prevent her body from coming in contact with his—to no avail. Her unruly heart only beat faster. She could not trust her own feelings, and it made her furious. His gentle smile only made matters worse.

"Do you find this amusing?" she said.

"Of course not. You are injured, which is not something I take lightly. I would never laugh at someone in dire circumstances. How heartless would that be? Do you consider me that much of a cad?"

Guilt overcame her, but she harbored resentment toward him still. "I doubt your compassion, Mr. Ramsdell. After all, you are capable of killing someone in cold blood."

He sighed, and she could feel his grip tightening as he carried her down the outside steps. "I'll have you know I didn't kill your brother. I don't care what you believe at this point, but that's the truth."

She couldn't believe him even if part of her wanted to. "If you did not, then who did?"

"I will find out," he said curtly and set her down on the soft cushions of the Blythe carriage.

"That is easier said than done."

"I know that." He sounded bitter.

"If you could not exonerate yourself before, what makes you believe you have a chance this time?"

"I have an excellent reason." He gave her a long stare. "But in the past I had no hope for my future. Now I can see some hope, a beam of light to inspire me."

"Poetry makes no impression on me," she replied.

"I realize that, but *I* intend to delve into the matter once more. As I said, I have an excellent reason."

She was afraid to ask him one word more.

Chapter 9

He joined her in the carriage, choosing to sit on the opposite seat, and the tension grew as they both avoided looking at each other. She sensed that he needed to talk more but could not find the words. Not that she would listen to him. A brittle vulnerability hung around them.

She had the power to cut him down at this moment, but try as she might, could not summon the coldness he so rightfully deserved. Taking a deep breath, she said, "I loved my brother very much."

"As did I," he said quickly. "We were friends to the very last, yet he sought more risk and more recklessness than was healthy. Something went awry along the path of our decadent lives."

"Oh? You drank too much brandy?"

"Well, yes, but there was something more sinister still. Some of Cedric's new friends were rather more wicked."

"What? Is that possible?" she asked, her voice scathing.

"Yes, unfortunately." Her tone didn't affect him. "They introduced us to something more dangerous than whiskey, and as I started to pull away, Cedric got more entrenched."

"Are you shifting the blame to other people he knew? I cannot accept that." She felt cold and inflexible inside, yet unsure of what to believe. "Nothing you say can soften me."

The carriage bumped across the cobblestones, and the tension between them made her stomach tighten with nausea. Her foot ached as it sat atop a cushion on the seat. Why had this happened? Cold sweat broke out on her forehead.

"Very well," he replied, his expression cool. "I am quite capable of shouldering my responsibilities."

"If you did, you would own up to your guilt and accept appropriate punishment."

He refused to answer, and the look he gave her made her shrink.

"I miss my brother every day," she said at last. "When we were young, Cedric always found ways to make boring days interesting, and his antics were too much for our tutors and governesses. His behavior drove away four of them in the Colonies. Then we came back here and he left for school. The days seemed endless after he departed, and the current governess took her revenge by pushing me to my limits. I did, however, learn a great deal." She smiled at the memory. "I resented every moment, but now I have her to thank, as she instilled in me a lasting passion for books. After Cedric went off to school we were never as close. I returned to the Colonies."

He nodded. "As with Charlie, I went in and out of Cedric's life. He was younger, and we had nothing in common in school. When he came to London upon graduating, we did our best to turn the town upside down. Strangely enough, I never knew him extremely well, and he had his own friends. When we happened to find ourselves in the same location, we recognized in each other a kindred spirit."

Lenore closed her eyes and sighed. "I wish he were back, but I know—"

"Wishful thinking is useless."

Sunlight slanted through the window as the coach turned a street corner. The golden light warmed her, lessening her emotional turmoil. "I know, yet you hope for the impossible."

"You only remember the good things."

"What's wrong with that?"

"Nothing, yet it's not the whole truth. He must have given you some worries."

"Edward is the one who worried the most. I was married and spent years on the Continent, in Vienna with my husband, until he passed on."

Silence hung for a moment, and it surprised her that he didn't ask her more questions about her life. But why should he? He was more interested in his own affairs, no doubt.

As if reading her thoughts, he said, "Cedric lived a rather selfish life, and so did I. Yet, I am a changed man since his tragic death. He never had that chance; he died as recklessly as he lived."

"Ah! You grew up, whereas Cedric died as immature as ever?" Her voice sounded scathing even to her own ears.

He gave her a long, cold look. "If you want to look at it that way, yes, I believe you're right. But I shan't take badly aimed barbs from you. You know very little about my life, so I ask you to refrain from judgment."

"High in the instep all of a sudden, eh?"

His mouth tightened to a thin line, and his eyes

took on a fire she'd never seen before. "Nothing can change the past and your sarcasm is pointless."

They weighed each other's strengths, like two pugilists ready to fight.

She felt herself weakening to a point, and curiosity took over. "Tell me exactly what happened that day," she said when the silence became unbearable.

"So that you can find faults with my actions on that ominous day? Hardly."

She shook her head. "No, I want to hear your side of the story."

"And compare it with the one the authorities told you?"

She shrugged her shoulders. "Perhaps. Someone is right, and I'm willing to hear your story."

"How gracious of you." He heaved a deep sigh and slapped his hand against his thigh. "It was a glorious morning, sunny, cool, a light wind. We had decided on the race a week before, and heavy bets had been laid at the clubs. As you probably know, high-perch phaeton races have been all the rage for some time, and we had decided—during an evening of excessive revelry—to beat the latest record from London to Brighton."

"High-perch phaetons are not safe for the kind of races you gentlemen are fond of."

"Be that as it may, we had two teams cheering us on. As I said, bets were heavy, and I was favored. I owned a better vehicle."

"Next you're going to say that someone sabotaged Cedric's phaeton, but he died from a bullet wound."

"Sabotage?" he asked, his voice tight with anger. "It never entered my mind."

"That was rather unfair of me," she admitted. "Go on."

"Even though it was early in the morning, Cedric

had imbibed a rather large quantity of brandy, and was somewhat unsteady on his pins."

"It was widely known you quarreled during the race, and possibly before."

"I was angry with him for drinking too much. For a phaeton race, we needed our wits about us. I also cautioned him that I wasn't going to spare my horses. It promised to be a difficult race. He only jeered at me, and got his hangers-on agitated on his behalf. If we had remained any longer, rotting tomatoes would have flown my way. The spectators were tipsy as well."

"You suspected you would win, didn't you?"

"I believed I had a chance, yes. Cedric was not himself, and I wonder if brandy was the only 'poison' he'd imbibed. As I told you before, something more sinister had entered his life."

Lenore looked into the abyss of the unknown. She didn't want to hear that Cedric had lived a life of deeper debauchery than she knew. Pressing her fingertips to her temples, she longed to push away the knowledge she hadn't been privy to before. She glanced at Mr. Ramsdell, who had become her tormentor in more ways than one, and her nerves seemed to have crawled to the very surface of her skin.

"I have only your word for it," she said. "You could easily make up a story about Cedric to impress me, to cast yourself in a better light."

He flung his head back against the squabs as if drowning in frustration. "I've no reason to do that. In fact, I don't care about your opinion of me, but I need to get to the truth."

She had no reply to that, and if he was trying to lie to her, he was succeeding. The look of urgency in his eyes could not be forced.

"Cedric started out ahead of me. I saw someone in the crowd who shouldn't have been there."

"Who?"

"I cannot say, until I have some real proof that he had a part in Cedric's death."

She couldn't believe what she heard. "So you are actually blaming someone else, even though you vowed you would not?"

"Someone else did kill him—I did not," he replied, his voice holding a colder edge.

She felt as if she were treading on dangerous ground. "The authorities made no mention of another man."

"They dismissed the idea as baseless. Still, no one saw me shoot. And I had not carried a pistol that day. They claimed I threw it away after the deed, but it was never found."

"Clever, aren't you?" Her head spun with all the information, and the horror of losing Cedric came back to haunt her. She'd tried to put it to rest and had mostly succeeded, yet new elements had been added this day, and it looked as if Cedric would not rest in peace until this matter had been solved. "If you're lying, I shall see to it that you end up destitute or in a dungeon."

"You don't understand, there is no proof."

"There are ways to ruin a man." As she said those words, a sharp twinge went through her foot.

"If that is your aim, you will find a way. But is it fair? Would you do that just on the assumption that I caused Cedric's death? Not even the authorities found—"

"You have powerful allies. Your grandfather is Lord Blythe, and I'm certain he knows many influential people. It would not be beyond him to ask a favor or two."

He leaned forward, his gaze penetrating her with a coldness that made her shiver. "I feel as if I'm talking in circles. Nothing I say seems to matter to you."

"Correct," she said with a nod of her head. "Until you provide some tangible proof, I shall not believe you. Others have managed to slither out of punishment for their sins, but I tell you, in the end, you'll pay."

He had nothing to say in reply to that. "At least we had a chance to exchange pleasantries," he said, his voice dripping with ice. "I don't know why I thought you'd be willing to listen to me."

"I don't owe you an ear, and I don't have to listen to your fabrications. That you would blame someone else is beyond the pale."

"I'm not placing *blame*, as you call it; I'm trying to discover the truth, something that is my right." He grew silent after those vehement words, and she could find nothing else to say. Perhaps he was right, but how would she know? Their argument hung heavily in the air between them, and she wished this ride had been finished a long time ago.

"We are almost there," he said, as if in response to her thoughts. "One of the longest journeys of my life."

"I did not ask for your company, and I certainly did not expect to injure my ankle because of you. Perhaps our family is cursed in your presence."

"That is ridiculous, and you know it, Mrs. Andrews."

"I don't know what to believe anymore."

"That's a thin excuse."

"You never give up, do you, Mr. Ramsdell?"

"Neither do you. I must say I'm disappointed. I had more confidence in you, but your stubbornness is exasperating."

She shivered, though the day was still warm. "I shall not deign to respond to that."

"As far as the accident goes, I'm very sorry that it happened, and the fact that I'm bringing you home is only what is expected—of a gentleman."

"Thank you," she said icily. "You could've sent one of the footmen to accompany me and we would've been spared this farcical interlude."

When the coach pulled up at her town house on Albemarle Street, Mr. Ramsdell stepped down in one fluid movement. It was obvious he longed to be gone. She moved her leg off the seat and another wave of pain went through it. Gritting her teeth, she moved halfway out of the door and into his waiting arms.

With three quick steps he had ascended the stairs to the front door, where Beaton waited, a frown between his eyebrows. "'Struth, what happened, ma'am?"

"I had a small accident, nothing to worry about. Just a sprained ankle. I shall be right as rain in a couple of days."

He shook his head as he looked at her swollen ankle, and made room for Ramsdell to enter. She resented his every step, but he shouldered through the first door, which was the front parlor. Without further ado, he set her down on the sofa and glanced around the aqua-and-white room, with its round mahogany table and chairs, and its softly upholstered sofas flanking the marble fireplace. Tall pink roses, a gift from Ludbank, adorned the table, and he threw a suspicious glance at those, as if knowing whom they were from.

He bowed. "I shall be off now. If there's anything else I can do for you, don't hesitate to contact me, Mrs. Andrews."

He sounded so indifferent that she doubted he

would ever do anything for her again. And good riddance, she thought as she inclined her head graciously.

"Good-bye, Mr. Ramsdell."

He left after giving her a hooded glance, and she was alone at last. Beaton entered and awaited her orders.

"Did you deliver my diary to the Rose Tearoom this morning?"

"I did, ma'am."

"Did you leave someone to spy on the comings and goings?"

"Two of the sharpest maids stayed for tea, and I told them not to leave until they found out whose servant came to pick up the journal. However"—he dragged out the words—"they got distracted."

"Distracted?"

"By choosing a variety of confits, ma'am. They got lost in the choices, and the lackey came and went, unnoticed. I shall sack them both presently."

Lenore started laughing, and her mirth took on almost hysterical proportions as all the tension of the day overwhelmed her.

Beaton pruned his mouth. "You find this amusing?"

She nodded, still convulsed. A painful stitch tightened in her side, and she gasped for air. "Don't sack them. The feast spread before them was probably too tempting to resist."

"Very well, ma'am."

She waved him away, suddenly tired of the whole debacle. "Never mind. The mystery may never be solved, but I'm dropping the matter of the diary. It has gone on long enough." She wiped her eyes and felt much better. "Send down Mildred, and one more thing: Did my brother call back?"

"No . . . but he said he would return here for dinner tomorrow."

"Is he *commanding* me to have dinner with him now? Very well, I can hardly run away." She glanced at her swollen ankle wrapped in a bandage. "Not for a while anyway."

He nodded, and left, closing the door very softly behind him.

She leaned her head back against the pillows and thought that this had surely been one of the worst days of her life. She did wish she had her diary in which to vent her frustration, but she'd decided she would start a new volume later.

Not too far away, Eric opened the diary. If he'd read her entry this morning, he would have laughed, but after spending such a grueling time with the writer of the pages, he could only groan with despair. She was a shrew of the worst kind, and he suspected that nothing but more aggravation could come out of pursuing a connection with her in the future. He should just let it go. Return the diary without anything but a good-bye, and leave it at that.

Yet he remembered the life-changing kiss in Vauxhall Gardens. How could he let her go? She was, under that bitter shell, a warm and delightful woman.

He sat down at his desk and composed a reply, possibly his last.

I'm thoroughly sorry that my entries in your journal have caused you despair and distress. What began as a lark has become something much more important. My aim has not been to hurt you, just make you think—though I know you'd reply that no one needs to remind you how to think. However, I need to confide in you now even if I'm only a lowly and opinionated man in your eyes. I believe you can advise me in this matter, and after that you shall have your diary back so that you can guard your privacy.

I'm in the worst quandary. You described the pain of being involved with a gentleman—your husband— who ultimately broke your heart and never worried about the effects of his actions on you. You would say that I act in the same manner, and perhaps you're right, but our previous discussion has opened my mind.

What has happened—I think—is that I've fallen in love with a lady who wants nothing to do with me. In fact, she loathes me, and I don't know how to show her that I'm not a complete ogre. I can hear you laugh now, and say you know why she loathes me, but I beg you to desist. I'm trying to learn how to really love someone and I realize it involves listening and under- standing and accepting. Though I understand other people's feelings, I fall short in the area of paying at- tention. But what do you do if the other person doesn't want to listen to you?

It was the truth, he thought. She wouldn't, or couldn't listen to him.

She did not believe in his innocence when it came to Cedric's death. If she ever found out that Eric had been the one to correspond in her journal, he would never have a chance to make amends with her.

Loneliness had put him in this precarious posi- tion. Blast and damn. For the first time in his life, a

woman had wholly entranced him and she was in
the middle of the most horrible ordeal of his life.
Why such fateful irony?

He returned to his writing.

*I can see from your entries that you think things
through, and I hope you can give me wise advice on
this matter. In fact, I don't hope, I know you can do it.
Please do not abandon me at so crucial a juncture. I
shall be forever grateful.*

He blotted the pages and reread what he'd written. This would surely touch her reluctant heart,
and he'd never met a female who could resist giving advice. Sighing, he leaned back in the wing chair
and braced his hands against the armrests. If she
replied with advice, he would know how to approach
her next—using her own tactics.

Chapter 10

"Beaton, you didn't discover who returned the diary on my doorstep?" Lenore asked, aggravated.

Beaton rubbed his hands in agitation, and his voice held a defensive note. "He left it yesterday afternoon, which we didn't expect. He changed his habit, and we cannot divine his plans ahead of time."

"Yes . . . I daresay. However, I am disappointed, and it worries me that the writer knows where I live. Somehow we ought to be able—"

"I know, ma'am! I shan't fail you again." His face turned mottled red with embarrassment.

Lenore weighed the journal in her hand. "There might not be a next time. I am heartily sick of this. The silly game is over."

Beaton could only bow to that, and he left the room with a quick step.

Lenore wondered what, if anything, the stranger had written as a good-bye. Probably very little.

She opened the well-worn pages and found a rather lengthy entry at the back. Frowning, she read the plea, and every word surprised her more. He was asking *her* for advice? He'd had nothing but contempt for her confidences.

Confused, she set the diary down. One fact bothered

her strangely: He had fallen in love with some lady. Her clandestine correspondent would now be shared with another, and she worried about it. That she had those selfish sentiments bothered her no end. She didn't even know the man, and she felt possessive just because he'd written scathing remarks to her? It was the outside of enough. There must indeed be something wrong with her—she ought to just wish him good luck and good riddance.

She drank the last of the coffee and ate the last piece of her buttered toast. She hadn't even touched the eggs or the ham, which perfumed the air with the scents associated with peaceful mornings. She still held the diary.

He wanted her advice. He must be demented if he believed she could help him.

She was a stranger, and yet he felt comfortable confiding in her. Mayhap he was inclined to look at her as a friend now after the written conversations they'd had. She was hard-pressed to forgive his previous entries, but heartless she was not, and she sensed a certain desperation in his last words. Sighing heavily, she stood and looked out the window onto the sunny street where carriages brought their occupants from one side of town to the next. Footmen ran back and forth with messages, and she wondered how many of them were on errands of an amorous nature. Many, she suspected. Infidelity was rampant in her social class, and she wondered where in London the writer sat or stood this day. Perhaps he knelt at the feet of his beloved. . .

She hobbled to her bedchamber, where Mildred was folding clean linen. She gave her mistress an appraising glance. "You look somewhat flustered, ma'am. Is anything the matter?"

"Nothing you have to concern yourself with, Mildred. I have missives to write this morning."

Mildred muttered something in reply, but Lenore paid no attention. She sat down at her escritoire and opened the journal to the last entry. After rereading it, she dipped her pen in the inkwell. After all, she could only give him her opinion.

At first I was amused at your sudden humility as you asked for my opinion, and then I realized you were serious. It is difficult for me to picture you, so fundamentally selfish, falling in love with someone. You would find a titillation of the senses, but would you know what it means to care for someone other than yourself? I seriously doubt it, and by your recent words you doubt it as well. I'm hard-pressed to find advice to give you in this matter.

It all hinges upon the woman with whom you've fallen in love. If she is tolerant, optimistic, and sympathetic, there might be a chance for happiness. You shall have to be the judge of her character, but I doubt you will recognize defects of your own.

And first you must learn to give someone of a gentle disposition a place of honor in your heart. I doubt very much you are capable of such a feat.

I've learned that you are an intelligent man, yet intelligence is not all that is necessary to succeed at love. To truly gain in sensitivity, you would have to give her your wholehearted affection, or lose your chance at winning her heart—unless she's a martyr. If you remain your imperious self, no lady in her right mind will flourish under your care. She would wilt like a flower without water.

If your good intention only lasts until you've said

*the vows at the altar, you will slowly lose her respect
and her love as she comes to understand the depth of
your selfishness. Truly, if she has an ounce of wisdom,
she'll perceive the truth of your character before she
marries you.*

*You'll have a long walk to reach the full under-
standing of love. We all do, and until love itself guides
us I daresay we will mistreat each other in a greater or
lesser fashion.*

*Perhaps you have come to a time in your life when
love truly means something at last.*

*I wish you luck in this endeavor, and I pray she is
kind and wise, as those are the only qualities that will
bring happiness to your union.*

Pleased, Lenore put down her quill and read
through what she'd written. He could only be satisfied
with this, and she wondered who the young woman
was. As far as she could tell, he'd been so very jaded,
and it would take somebody truly enchanting to light
a spark in his heart. Yet she worried that he would just
flatten a tender heart. If the woman was very young,
she might not have the strength and experience to
stand up to him.

Lenore knew her correspondent rather well by
now, but it startled her to remember that she didn't
know his identity.

She had advised him at length about love. Such ready
words, she thought, yet what did she know about it? She
had learned what love was not with Ronald, and the lesson had been painful. Before his betrayal, she had flung
herself heart and soul into romantic love, and with the
buoyancy of youth, believed that perfection was possible. The disappointment had been deep, and her

innocence had been lost forever, but wisdom had grown in its place.

She got up and rolled her neck, which had stiffened in the last half hour. She would send Beaton out first thing in the morning, and this time he *had* to discover the identity of her secret correspondent. Her curiosity was now too great to set aside.

In the late afternoon, a knock sounded on her door, and Mildred stepped inside. "Your brother has arrived."

"Edward is early." She hurried to button up the buttons on the bodice of her pearl gray silk gown. Her hair still had to be arranged, and she sat down at her dressing table, where Mildred set to work with the silver-backed brush.

Her dark hair shone with the strokes and threatened to fly away. Sunlight from the window brightened the room with gold and turned more orange by the minute as the afternoon lengthened. Lenore dabbed some powder on her cheeks and placed pearl earrings in her ears.

Letting her brother wait downstairs—fuming, no doubt—she took her time to get ready. She had no desire to argue with him tonight, and she longed for a quiet moment to sort through her thoughts and feelings. Peace had evaded her for a long time now, and she needed it badly.

Edward looked elegant in a black evening coat, starched linen, a perfect neck cloth tied in the mathematical knot, and silk knee breeches. "Have you been invited to a royal soirée, Edward?"

He smiled. "Hardly, my dear sister, but I have been invited to a late supper at Lord Alvanley's. A gathering of cronies."

"Ah! Gentlemen drinking brandy and playing cards."

"You look very elegant yourself, " he replied. "I assume you have been invited somewhere too." He glanced at her bandaged foot and the crutches. "Then again, perhaps not."

She shook her head.

Edward helped her into the dining room and set her down by the window. He poured himself a glass of sherry while they waited for the table to be set. He handed Lenore a glass, too, and they watched the street through the window. Birds bickered along the eve of the house across the street, and a weather vane creaked in the wind. The traffic had thinned out as evening fell, and the servants had returned to those they served to prepare for dinner.

"Lenore, I know you prefer your independence, and I will not argue with you on that. But Ludbank has made his intentions clear, and we're waiting for you, m'dear. However, I shall not force you, even if I'd like to."

"It hurts me to think you'd like to force me."

"Only because I worry about you."

He took a deep breath and drank deeply from the sherry glass. His voice took on a steely inflection. "It has come to my attention that you spent yesterday in the company of Eric Ramsdell."

"I don't know what you heard, but most of the time I spent with Lady Blythe, all against my own wishes, with my foot propped on a pillow. However, I find her to be a rather pleasant woman."

"I found out that Ramsdell took you home, *alone* in the carriage, and then carried you inside the house."

She nodded. "Correct. There is nothing unseemly about that. I sprained my ankle badly, and he was at fault."

Edward's face turned red. "How could you put yourself in a position where you encountered him in the first place? I asked you to stay away from him, and the next thing I know, you have become even more entangled."

"Entangled? You are exaggerating." Lenore felt anger rising within her, and she had no desire to deal with her brother and his unreasonable demands tonight.

"Our worst enemy entered this house, his arms around you, and you say I am exaggerating?" His hand trembled as he set down his glass on a tiny marble-topped table.

"Yes, he did, and yes, it is an exaggeration. I couldn't walk without assistance, and I would never allow Beaton to carry me inside. He would have had an apoplexy, and I would never let any of the footmen touch my form—unless I was dying."

"But you would let *him*?"

"It was only for a short time. He set me down and left. Nothing more. We had no further interaction, and since he was partially to blame for the accident, he took his responsibility seriously and took me home."

"I'm sure he did, and tried to whitewash himself in the process."

"You are overly suspicious," she said. Ramsdell *had* tried to whitewash himself, Lenore thought, but she might have tried the same thing in his position.

"I have grounds."

"That is neither here nor there, Edward. Nothing he says can change my opinion of him, or the crime he committed."

Edward clamped his hand around her arm as if to make a point. "I don't want it to be said around town that my sister hobnobs with her brother's killer. Cedric would turn in his grave—"

"He would not! He would laugh at the irony of the situation." She pulled herself free and held out her glass toward Edward. "Please refill my glass. The pain is quite excruciating in my ankle and the sherry makes it easier to bear."

"I see," he replied grimly, and went to the decanter.

"No, you do not. You think of our reputation more than you think about my well-being. If I had broken my neck, you would have worried about the cause of my accident, and how it would look to the world."

Edward groaned with frustration, and Beaton, carrying a pitcher of lemonade through the door, gave him a discreet sideways glance.

"Your flippant remarks infuriate me, Lenore."

"Well, a stickler like you, Edward, is shocked when someone—"

"I am not!" he interrupted. "I have to think of the family. It's horrifying enough that Cedric lost his life the way he did." He choked on his last words, and Lenore placed her hand over his as he sat down beside her, fresh sherry in hand.

"Calm down, Edward."

"I cannot."

"No matter how you worry, Cedric will never come back, and he wouldn't give a fig for the family name. Just remember how he really was—he didn't care what we thought about his scrapes, and if he had lived any longer, he would have done worse."

"Yes . . . I daresay you're right."

"You cannot change the past, Edward. Just let it go."

Edward hung his head. "That is the hardest part. He's forever gone, and it haunts me more every day."

"Some evidence is bound to come to light sooner or later, and Eric Ramsdell will be punished for the crime he committed." Every word she had just uttered weighed on her, and she realized she wished that Ramsdell was innocent. That knowledge made her spirits sink even lower, because she couldn't see how she could get closer to the man, innocent or not.

"Just stay away from Ramsdell, Lenore."

"Edward, you have little faith in me. It always astounds me that you feel you have to berate me for my behavior."

"You are . . . so unpredictable and that worries me, Lenore. You don't care about convention. In that sense, you are like Cedric."

"I do," she said thoughtfully, "and if you paid attention, you would see that I've never done anything to besmirch the family name."

He puffed out his red cheeks and stared at her. "Very well, I take your point. Just stay away from Eric Ramsdell."

She swallowed her anger. "I never asked for his help."

"You could have sent word to me."

"You're not my keeper, Edward."

Silence fell after that and she looked toward the table, where the meal awaited them.

"I ordered your favorite—veal and truffles in a wine sauce."

He smiled then and rubbed his hands together in delight. "I've worked up quite an appetite."

The next day her ankle felt somewhat better even if it throbbed every time she set her foot down. She had kept cold compresses wrapped around it, and the swelling had gone down a fraction. Spending the morning inside bored her, as the weather was sunny and warm. To her relief she received a brief missive from Belinda, asking her to paint in the park, as they did every week. She accepted gratefully, even if her ankle hurt. It would be more painful to brood alone at home than to suffer twinges in her ankle as she jostled back and forth in the carriage.

Mildred helped her don a pale yellow muslin gown with a white fringed silk sash. She wore a straw hat to protect her face from the sun, and when she bent down to put on her half boots, she found the foot still too swollen. Very well, she would just wear her white stocking and place her foot on the pillow.

Beaton ordered the footmen to load her painting materials and a basket of food and wine, and then she set off with two of the servants to aid her. Belinda was already in the park when they arrived. This time she'd set up her easel at the opposite side of the pond and had already begun to paint a group of ducks feeding at the edge of the pond. She waved to Lenore and continued her quick brushstrokes to capture the ducks before they could swim away.

Lenore felt tired and out of sorts, but sitting outdoors with the sun on her back cheered her. The servants set up her easel close enough to Belinda that she could keep up a conversation with her friend.

She told Belinda what had happened to her ankle and her close encounter with Eric Ramsdell, and she mentioned Lady Blythe's kindness and Edward's anger.

Belinda's blue eyes widened with amazement. "And all of this happened since the day before yesterday? I saw you and you went back home—supposedly."

"Life can change very quickly." Lenore dotted some

oil paint onto her palette and set to creating the image of a weeping willow at the edge of the pond. Her hand was unsteady and she found it difficult to paint the narrow green leaves and the shadow they cast on the blue water of the pond. She stared into the blue space above, and she lost her concentration. By now, the stranger who had become her confidant of sorts must have received her journal.

Eric read the entry, his eyes clouding over with sudden tears. It hurt to cry. It had been so long since he cried, and he resented the emotion, yet he knew he needed it.

Every word she'd written rang true, but he didn't want to hear a single one of them.

Of course he knew how to love and no one had to tell him how to treat a lady.

Least of all the opinionated man-hater who had authored the diary in his lap. Still, part of him longed to meet her but . . . his heart heavy, he remembered that she would never talk to him again willingly, let alone allow him anywhere near her.

Blasted nuisance! He had never asked for this. Why would the lady for whom he'd developed a *tendre* be so completely unattainable? He rose from his grandfather's chair behind the desk in the library and went to send an order to the stables for his horse. He needed to get out, to take some action to change his life.

His heart squeezed with pain, and a gnawing worry troubled his mind. He went upstairs and dressed for riding. His fingers trembled as he buttoned his coat, and his head still ached from crying. If he shed any more tears, he would end up a puddle on the floor.

He rode through town, down past Haymarket, and to seedy lodgings where he hadn't been for a long time. Some dry leaves from last year rustled down the cobbled street, and a cool breeze pulled at his coat as he climbed out of the saddle and asked an urchin to watch his horse with the promise of a penny. Clenching his teeth, he knocked on a brown painted door, and after an ungodly wait, he heard shuffling footsteps within. A manservant opened the door a crack. His narrow face showed an unhealthy pallor, and his teeth were broken, his clothes patched.

"Yarrow, I want to see Sir Winton."

"He's not at home, Mr. Ramsdell."

Eric pressed his elbow hard against the door and forced it open. "Of course he is. Still sleeping off the laudanum, I'm sure."

Yarrow protested, but his feeble strength was nothing compared to Eric's. The hallway was gloomy and had not been aired out for weeks. Curtains were drawn in the front room and in the bedroom, where he knew he would find Sir Winton.

He did. Sir Winton groaned when Eric shook his shoulder. The man reeked of dirty linen and an unwashed body. Eric recoiled and stared at the emaciated face on the soiled pillow. Sir Winton badly needed a haircut, but it was unlikely he could afford any niceties at this juncture. All his money, whatever he had left, went to feed his addiction, which would end his days soon enough if he continued.

"Get up! It's well past noon."

"Ramsdell?" His voice was hoarse and his eyes bloodshot. "Damn you to hell! Get out of here."

Eric gripped his nightshirt and half lifted him out of bed. "Wake up, I need to speak with you."

"Get out!" The man flailed his thin arms but couldn't focus enough to get a grip on Eric. He slumped, and would have fallen back onto the lumpy mattress if Eric hadn't held him up.

"Pull yourself together, Winton. How low can you sink?"

Sir Winton sat on the edge of the bed, his head slumping between his shoulders and his hands hanging loosely between his knees. His oily strands of brown hair hung in disarray around his face.

"Where is your pride, Winton? Look at you."

"What are you doing here, Ramsdell?"

Eric stood over him, boiling with frustration. "I want you to know I haven't given up on the truth. As long as I live, I won't give up."

"What are you talking about?" Sir Winton asked, his voice whiny. "I have no business with you."

"Guilt. Yours. As I said, I'll find out the truth."

Sir Winton didn't reply. His gaze moved around the room, probably searching for the claret bottle on the lowboy. Most of the contents were already gone, but he obviously needed something to strengthen himself.

Disgusted, Eric handed him the bottle, and Sir Winton grabbed hold of it as if it were a buoy. He tilted the bottle to his pale lips and drank.

"I daresay nothing has changed around here, Winton. You're as damned as ever, and with that last blow to your finances, you've finally gone to pot. No way out now, except the cent-per-centers—or death."

Sir Winton growled and gave Eric a glance full of hatred. "If you're here to rub salt in my wounds, you've come in vain. Nothing you say or do will change the foul taste in my mouth, and I don't care one whit for

your mission, whatever it is. As far as I know, we have nothing more to say to each other."

He threw himself back down against the pillows, one arm shielding his eyes. Anger welled up in Eric, and he pushed away the other man's arm and stared straight into the cloudy, troubled eyes. "You might not care, but I do. You killed Cedric, and I shall find a way to prove it. You know and I know the truth."

Sir Winton gave a faint smile, one that said he didn't care at all.

A cold tingle went down Eric's spine, and he felt the familiar hopelessness that had haunted him before.

"I don't give a blasted penny for your opinion, Ramsdell. You will never prove me guilty, nor will anyone else. You must live with the guilt because you were there, and the world judged you, not me." He poked a thin finger into Eric's chest. "You can dig for clues all you want, and you won't find a thing." He wheezed a laugh, and Eric longed to slap him, challenge him to a duel, but that wouldn't help at all.

"I'll find that old filly of yours, Miss Sharp."

"She'll have nothing to tell you."

"So where is she? Have you hidden her away?"

Sir Winton shook his head feebly. "Where would I find the strength, you fool? I have no idea where she is these days."

"You treated her with utter contempt."

"Just as she deserved. A doxy is always a doxy."

"She still deserved human consideration." Eric stood over the other man, fury boiling within him.

Sir Winton chuckled. "The trouble here is not I, but you. Your conscience is bothering you, because you treated the doxies with the same contempt. I don't have a conscience, so the past doesn't bother me."

"If it didn't, you wouldn't soil yourself with filth like this." Eric flicked the man's dirty sleeve. "You have no self-respect. You have nothing."

"It means nothing to me anymore." Sir Winton cackled. "Damn you to hell."

Fury in his eyes, Eric turned on his heel and left the room.

Chapter 11

Eric rode along the shaded sandy path of the park. His temper had calmed down, and he could breathe normally again. He recalled every vivid detail of nights he'd spent on the town with Cedric, how they hadn't cared about the upheaval they left behind as they brawled in low taverns, used women, and instigated outrageous bets at gentlemen's clubs.

Sir Winton had never avoided a bet or a card game, but Cedric had become his nemesis. Sir Winton had not been able to quell his resentment. Eric sighed, a feeling of sorrow in his heart, as he recalled the fateful events, and how Cedric had gained a deadly enemy on one night of card games. Cedric hadn't cared of course; it was all of an evening to him, one of many.

Sir Winton had lost everything.

The event had left a bad taste, and some of their cronies had wondered if Cedric had cheated or if Sir Winton was so drunk that his mental faculties had been shattered.

Eric didn't want to speculate, and it still pained him to remember. This had, in his opinion, been the night that triggered all the evil to come later. A bird, startled out of a tree, flew past his head, and he came out of his reverie. It had been a while since all of these memories had been created, but his life had stood still since then.

He rode along the path slowly, noticing very little around him, though the grass was so green it was almost iridescent, and the sky so blue it glowed. He did notice the warmth on his back and it revived him after the unnerving encounter with Sir Winton. Truth to tell, the man looked like he wasn't far from the grave, Eric thought. If he went, he would take the truth with him.

Eric rounded a curve in the lane, and a pond spread out before him, surrounded with stands of oaks and elms. People picnicked in the grass and wandered among the trees, chatting. He envied their closeness, but pushed away the sentiment. Wasted energy, he thought, and scoffed at himself for such weakness.

To his surprise, he noticed familiar faces near the pond. Two ladies had set up their easels to capture the scene before them. Lenore looked beautiful in her yellow dress, and he wondered how her ankle was. If she was abroad this sunny day, it could not be too bad.

Mrs. Chandler seemed completely absorbed in her painting. Lenore looked up and noticed him as he rode closer. She placed her hand to her throat and he could almost hear her fearful gasp. Her eyes filled with despair, and he wished he'd taken another path. Her rejection was just another burden to bear.

He lifted his beaver hat. "Good morning," he said. "I don't mean to intrude, but how is your ankle today, Mrs. Andrews?"

He didn't really expect an answer, but she spoke. "Better, thank you." If her voice had been any stiffer, it would have broken, he thought.

She gave him a quick glance that told him to leave,

but it only served to ignite his ire, which had been boiling close to the surface as it was.

"I am glad to hear it. Beautiful day for painting. Just the right light." He felt silly for speaking such platitudes, but he had a right to be here, just as she did.

"I'd rather you not speak with me."

Mrs. Chandler had laid down her tools and was staring at him. "Did you hear her? Just leave us alone."

Eric fought his wave of anger. "As far as I know, this is a public park and I have not trespassed on your territory in any way."

"Except for breaking the code of gentlemanly behavior," Lenore said.

"I have said nothing that could be interpreted as an insult or a rude remark. In fact, I have done nothing that would warrant such callous treatment from you. The code of *politesse* goes both ways, does it not? Or it should, if the world were fair—which it rarely is."

Lenore put a hand to her mouth in a bout of sudden mirth, and it took him by surprise. "Isn't he the outside of enough," she said to her friend. "First he breaks every rule of behavior, and then he expects us to applaud his conduct. The incredible nerve of the man!"

"You promised Edward you would not speak with this man again," Mrs. Chandler warned, her gaze sending daggers at him.

"Pooh, Edward is not my keeper. Never has been and never will be," Lenore said, and Eric let out his breath. He hadn't noticed he'd been holding it.

"I admire people who don't buckle under to others' opinions," he said.

"I would never buckle under to yours," she said, her voice short.

"I have no doubt. You're not one easily swayed." He

wished she were a little more tolerant of him, but at least she hadn't completely shut him out. He admired her inner strength and her nerve.

"I like to paint too, but I haven't found the peace to apply myself wholeheartedly lately. It takes concentration," he said, trying to lengthen the conversation. He longed to stay, to find a way to break down her wall. He'd never felt so vulnerable, and his situation was more painful than anything he had experienced in the past.

Love makes you weak, he thought. She could just push home the knife any second, and he could do nothing to defend himself. If his name were cleared, would she accept his friendship then? His thoughts dared not touch on the possibility of a courtship, but, yes, he wanted to kiss her seductive mouth again and hold her close. It was as if she could read his desire, and her gaze pierced him with a knowing look that was both intimate and disturbing.

Dear Lenore, he wanted to write in her diary, *I have fallen completely in love with you. I want to hold you so tenderly that you'd never wish to leave,* he thought.

"What do you paint besides horses?" she asked, her voice faraway.

He started, and his horse sidestepped under him as if tired of standing and staring at nothing. He pulled in the reins to keep control. "Landscapes, mostly, but old ruins and castles fascinate me also."

"They are difficult to depict, and so are animals, especially dogs. I won't even try." Lenore put down her brush, and Mrs. Chandler gave her a glance through narrowed eyes. A warning was coming, he thought, but to his surprise, she didn't say anything. She went back to her painting.

He decided to dismount, and when no one protested, he tied the horse to a tree and strolled to the water's edge. Ducks paddled in the pond grass in search of food, and bobbed up and down without any concern for their surroundings. They knew nothing about the tension he was feeling.

"You should not be here, Mr. Ramsdell," Lenore said.

He had a flip remark on his tongue, but he swallowed it. He gave her a curt nod. "I know it may be in bad taste to say this, and unacceptable as well, but I like talking to you," he confessed.

Her cheeks reddened, and she looked away.

"I daresay you have nothing to say to that, Mrs. Andrews."

"I should be flattered I suppose, but a compliment coming from you is—how shall I say it—sullied somehow."

Her words hurt him, but he smiled. "I must find a better way to converse with you. Perhaps you can tell me what you like."

"No. I am not supposed to speak with you."

"I thought we were past that point. I'm here. We have kept up a conversation in the last few minutes without the earth opening up and swallowing me."

She nodded. "You're right. I shouldn't harp on convention when I fly in the face of it constantly." She stood, but abruptly remembered her ankle and fell back onto the stool again. Waving at the servants sitting in the grass by the coach, she asked them to unpack the lunch basket and watched them spread out a blanket. She motioned toward the square green cloth on the grass. "Please sit down, Mr. Ramsdell. If I cannot get rid of you, you might as well make yourself at home, or forever skulk at the edges of my social life."

She did not have to ask him twice.

"Lenore!" Mrs. Chandler still looked angry, but her expression had softened with resignation. "Edward will never forgive you."

"I don't care. This is none of his concern."

With a brisk stride, Eric went to help Lenore.

"Thank you." She leaned on his arm and hobbled along to the blanket. He felt the soft skin of her arm under his fingers, and he wanted to close his eyes and stay this close forever, near her.

"Mind where you walk," she said as he tripped on the edge of the blanket. She laughed, a soft, melodious sound. "Are you asleep?"

"I was dreaming about you," he whispered, and she laughed even more.

Mrs. Chandler gave them a glance of outrage, but when the servants put out the food on the blanket, covered dishes with cold chicken and quail, marinated vegetables, cake, and wine, she put her paints down and joined them. She sat as far away from them as she could.

"What if someone sees us?" she whispered. "You shall be forever condemned, Lenore."

"I am already, don't you think? I believe the ladies Herrington and Wedge just drove by on their daily outing, and they are the worst gossips. This event will be in the newssheet tomorrow, and my brother will oppress me with the severest set-down of the century."

"Newssheets? Hardly, but whoever is left in London will know," Mrs. Chandler said, her voice tinged with discomfort. "Adam will be livid that I'm associating with you."

"Blame everything on me, Belinda. He won't be surprised, but he'll forbid you to keep our friendship."

"Yes, Adam would not be surprised; he says you are a bad influence on me." Mrs. Chandler relaxed her stiff posture on the blanket and spread her light blue skirt around her. She shielded her face from the sun with her frilly parasol and sighed deeply.

Eric thought she looked lonely, and he suspected she had never experienced such ordinary bliss as picnics in the park with someone who loved her. He understood the feeling, yet he'd never lacked for female company. He had enjoyed them, but no one had ever touched his heart like Mrs. Andrews. Lenore. He loved her name.

"May I call you by your first name?" he asked her.

She blushed again, and lowered her eyes. "Yes . . . you may. Formality can be so stifling."

"Then call me Eric, if you will." He leaned back on one elbow against the blanket. "And I would like to hear about your life, from the very beginning—everything."

"Are you going to *listen* all the time it takes to tell you about it?" She looked incredulous.

"Why not? Isn't love about listening and understanding? And actually paying attention?"

Her eyes widened, and the movement of her open fan slowed. "Your words have a familiar ring."

"Familiar? I don't know what you're talking about. Caring involves truly knowing the other person, am I correct?"

"Yes . . . of course, you're completely right. I couldn't have said it better myself." She sounded baffled. "But—from what I understand, you care about no one but yourself."

"That is unfair, especially since you don't know me very well. All you know is what you've heard about me."

"I have watched you . . . eh, Eric, on the occasions we've met, and you have not impressed me with a great capability for listening, or accepting."

Mrs. Chandler coughed hard, her face averted. She hid herself from them using her parasol as a shield.

"No need to laugh at me, Mrs. Chandler," he chided.

An awkward silence fell. Eric shifted back to a sitting position.

"I was not laughing," Mrs. Chandler said as she regained her voice. "Just coughing."

"You are both laughing at me," he accused, knowing he was right. "I reveal myself, and all I get is scorn."

"Don't be silly," Lenore said. "Are you sincerely suggesting that you're a good listener?"

He nodded, feeling like a fraud. "I try."

"Why would you find my past interesting?" Lenore prodded.

"Because I am . . . because I find you fascinating," he blurted out, meaning every word. "You are what would make me listen and, well, learn." He threw a guilty glance at her, but also one at Mrs. Chandler, who had heard every word.

"Lenore," Mrs. Chandler said, tension in her voice, "perhaps we should return home before you get too deeply involved in this conversation."

The servants filled glasses with sherry and passed them around.

"Yes, perhaps we should," Lenore said, accepting a glass , but she made no effort to move.

"You are not thinking clearly," Mrs. Chandler said. "I am."

"This is folly. You know Edward will do something drastic to punish you."

"Of course," Lenore said and sipped her sherry. "But

I'll find a way to handle him. He'll try to bundle me off to the spinster aunts, but he cannot force me to go." She pointed toward the dishes. "Have some meat and bread, Belinda. We shall be home in due time, and we'll wonder why we hurried from this bucolic spot—or worried. There is no harm in sharing an innocent picnic in the park."

"We still have our reputations to consider," Belinda said with some asperity.

Lenore's cheeks turned red with embarrassment or high spirits. Eric wasn't sure, and there was nothing he could say, but he didn't want her to leave. She lay back against the blanket, and a servant placed a pillow under her injured foot.

"I haven't finished my painting," Lenore said and drank some more sherry. "I want to stay here a bit longer."

"There's always another day," Mrs. Chandler said, clearly impatient.

"Dearest friend, if you are that worried, please remove yourself and I shan't hold it against you."

Mrs. Chandler threw a glance at Eric. "But then you'll be alone with this *man*, and I shall worry about you no end. As it is, I am acting as your chaperone."

Lenore laughed, and Eric's breath caught in his throat at the sound of her merriment. Indeed, this encounter was utter foolishness, but he couldn't help himself. Courtesy required that he remove himself. He did not want Lenore's brother to make her life difficult, but he realized he didn't have the strength to leave. He could only sit here and listen to her laugh, even if only minutes remained. When had such weakness ever overcome him? Perhaps the very first time he looked into her eyes at the Rose Tearoom, and she hadn't really seen him.

He automatically accepted a plate of food when Lenore served it to him. It could have been sawdust for all he cared; he noticed only the graceful movements of her hands, and the seductive curve of her neck. Lenore gave him a teasing glance, her eyes glittering.

"Aren't you going to protest Belinda's derogatory comment about you?"

"Why?"

"She did not give you a compliment."

"I have heard worse, and I'm sure she is only trying to protect you. But it's clear to me you like to play with fire, don't you, Lenore?"

"Why would you say that?"

"If not, you would not be here with me today or even acknowledge me. You would run away, if it came to that."

She pointed at her elevated foot. "As you know, I cannot hobble, let alone run, even if I wanted to."

"Do you want to?" he asked softly, adoring her.

She blushed deeply, and he could tell she wanted to stay, which made his heart beat faster.

Belinda looked more uncomfortable every minute. She finished her food in a hurry and returned to her painting, as if that would remove her from any hint of scandal. She angled her easel so that she had her back turned toward them. The stiffness of her spine conveyed profound disapproval.

Lenore noted his contemplation of Mrs. Chandler's back, and she said, "Please do not worry about her. As you say, she is concerned about me and what will happen."

"She is a loyal friend, and friends protect each other."

"If you had been Cedric's friend, you would have protected him."

That statement hung explosively between them, and there was no way to soften the raw truth. He had no more defense in him.

"Lenore, Cedric *was* my friend, always. At the end, he was slipping away from me because I did not approve of his actions, but that was his choice."

"I agree," she said with a sigh, "but this issue will always stand between us and forever take away any chance of companionship."

"Would you like, er, companionship with me?" he asked, his whole world hanging on what she would say.

She shrugged. "I don't know why I said that. I do find you fascinating, but I know your character, alas."

"You can't change another person."

"But the truth is the truth, and it cannot be hidden, however much you hope to accommodate me." She studied his face until he replied.

"I accept myself, yet I know my limitations," he said at last.

"At least you are honest," she said with a smile.

"That's a great start." He set his glass down on the empty plate to prevent it from falling over on the soft blanket. "Now, tell me your life story."

"It was nothing much out of the ordinary except for the years I spent in the Colonies with my aunt. The people there don't set much store on convention, and they flourish nonetheless. Their society is not as rigid as ours. The rather savage surroundings called for ingenuity and bravery rather than convention."

"How did you come to live in the Colonies?"

"My mother was born in Virginia, on a tobacco plantation. My grandfather was the youngest son of Lord

Erskine—the black sheep of the family, if you will. Yet, he made rather a success of himself. I'm certain my father must have loved my mother greatly to marry her. According to society standards he should've made a much better match."

"In other words, you are rather like him, as you dare to fly in the face of convention." He longed to pull her into his arms and kiss every inch of her face. He longed to press his nose against her neck.

"I don't like it when someone forbids me to do something. I have done nothing wrong, and I deserve trust from those closest to me."

He nodded. "I would agree"

She leaned back against the pillows and shaded her eyes with her hand. "Isn't it a beautiful day?"

"Yes . . . are you changing the subject?"

"What if I were? No matter how long we talk about this, nothing will change the fact of what happened that day Cedric died. It will stand as it is, but I'm talking to you . . ."

"Because?" He wanted to hear her say that she really wanted, or needed, to talk to him.

"Because I have windmills in my head." She giggled and raised her glass of sherry. "There's no other explanation."

Disappointment sat like a lump in his chest. He drank some more wine as one of the servants refilled his glass. Was he hoping for forgiveness?

Even if she wanted to forgive him, she couldn't. He should be out raking through the evidence of Cedric's murder, not sitting here on a blanket in the park making eyes at a woman with whom he was smitten. Had it only been a few weeks since he met her? It seemed so much longer. Thanks to her diary, she was immensely more familiar to him than he was to her.

The diary. Guilt started eating at him as he thought about the subterfuge. He had never dreamed that she would in any way become important to him. Responding to her entries had been an amusing way to make his days move faster. If she ever found out . . . He pushed away the thought.

"Truth is the most important thing in a friendship," she said as if reading his mind.

"Indeed, it cannot be emphasized enough," he replied feebly and emptied his glass with one gulp.

She leaned closer to him as she angled her elbow on the pillows. "Tell me, what makes a lady interesting to you?"

He touched the tip of her nose with his finger. "No, you tell me what makes a gentleman special in your eyes."

"I asked first," she said, pouting.

He thought for a moment. "Well, then. Someone who has a sense of her own worth and shows it. She's not afraid to speak her mind, or *have a mind* of her own. So many females have no opinion about anything, and I find that tiresome. She is loving and has a sense of humor. Her character is mature."

Lenore giggled. Evidently the sherry was taking effect. "This paragon sounds very old and serious. A matron of uncertain years."

"Not at all!" he cried. "She is lovely, with a body as lithe as that of a gazelle—like yours, well, when your ankles are in order."

"You flatter me," she replied, her eyes glittering with something he couldn't quite read. Did compliments annoy or excite her?

"You asked the question in the first place, and I have answered truthfully."

"Yes . . . very well."

"It is your turn."

"I admire integrity and wisdom in a gentleman, maturity tempered with a sense of adventure and delight."

"Don't forget trust," he chided as he recalled her journal entries.

"You mean truth?"

"No, trust. You do not trust easily."

Her eyes narrowed. "How would you know?"

"Simple enough. You don't trust me."

"I have a perfectly good reason for not trusting you." Her voice held a cold edge.

"I understand," he said with a sigh. "I was just thinking that I'm a fool, sitting here like a moonling with starlight in my eyes when I should be thinking of clearing my name." He stood in one fluid movement. "In fact, I must set to work, or be forever haunting you on the edges of the parks. As it is, we can never stand together in front of society."

A cloud crossed over her face. "In that, you hear no argument from me. Part of me hopes you succeed; part of me hopes you will pay for what you did."

He smiled faintly. "Well, you have no difficulty speaking your mind, that much is true."

She laughed. "I shall not give you false hope. As it is, I have no intention of ever speaking with you again. You might call this encounter a quirk of Fate, nothing more."

"How hurtful you can be with your ruthless adherence to truth. Let me add to my description of the perfect female. She possesses graciousness, gentleness, and compassion. In fact, I put those traits before all others."

Her eyes widened, and a flash of doubt shaded them. "I understand, and I agree. However, I was not raised in a polite world where gentleness was valued."

"You are making excuses," he said, suddenly tired.

"No, I am not. I am who I am."

Why did he even bother? He noticed a stubborn look on her face, and knew she would defend herself despite her declaration of the opposite. "Very well. So you are," he said. "But you shall never find true graciousness if you always have to be right."

She struggled to her feet. Her face turned red with the effort of walking without a crutch or a helping hand, and when he tried to give her his arm, she pushed him away. Annoyance impelled her to hobble to the edge of the pond and sit down on a tussock. He stared in surprise as she rolled down her stockings, removed her bandage, and put her bare feet into the water.

Belinda gasped at such wanton behavior, and Eric felt uncomfortable, as if Lenore had done this to provoke him. Perhaps he had pushed her too far.

Lenore laughed at them. "Am I shocking you?"

Belinda put down her brush and ran to her friend's side. "Oh, Lenore. You mustn't," she hissed.

Eric was embarrassed, yet amused. He had not expected outrageous behavior from Lenore, but at the same time he wasn't surprised. He went to stand next to them. Lenore splashed her feet, and a strand of pond grass stuck between her toes.

"I daresay Virginia ladies think nothing of taking their stockings off in public," he said dryly.

Belinda looked daggers at him, but he ignored her. "You mustn't stare at her legs," she demanded.

"I have seen nothing," he lied.

Lenore kept laughing, and he suspected she had

drunk too much sherry. "If you wish to shock me," he said, "you have failed. You are only making a spectacle of yourself."

"You are not my master," Lenore said. "My feet were very hot and my ankle throbbed, and I feel much better now."

"Your aim was only to provoke," he said. "Your rebellion has its roots in anger, but your act is ill-chosen as it serves no purpose."

"Except for cooling my feet." She lifted her chin in defiance. "If it bothers you, please leave."

"Lenore, where are your manners?" Belinda asked, her shoulders stiffening with exasperation.

"I was graciously asking him to leave—"

"Desist," he shouted. "None of this has an effect on me. You seem to forget that I have seen much more than bare feet where the fair sex is concerned."

Both women gasped at his bold remark, and Lenore's cheeks turned even redder, whereas Mrs. Chandler paled.

"Sir, you have overstepped the bounds of polite conversation," Mrs. Chandler said.

He pointed at Lenore's bare feet. "Just as you have. I care nothing for what you do to shock me, but *you* should care. What if Ludbank hears of this? He'll never marry you now."

He thought Lenore would protest, he hoped she would, but she didn't say anything, only stared straight ahead, anger stiffening every line of her body.

"I for one have had enough of this charade," Mrs. Chandler said, looking most distressed.

He bowed. "It was a delightful picnic, ladies."

Without another word, he unhitched his horse, swung himself into the saddle, and rode away.

Chapter 12

"Why did you allow this to happen, Lenore?" asked Belinda. "You shall be the talk of the town."

"Frankly, I don't care." Lenore brushed some stray pieces of grass from her gown and let one of the lackeys help her back to her chair in front of her easel.

Belinda followed and stood beside her. Her friend stared at her, making her uncomfortable.

"Why?" Belinda asked. "And why are you so angry? There's no reason to behave in an uncouth fashion. I've never seen you like this. I believe you have developed a *tendre* for that villain, and probably only to annoy your brother."

"That is untrue!" Lenore cried. "I would not love Eric Ramsdell if he were the last man on earth."

"Oh—balderdash and you know it. You protest too much."

"I shall not speak with him again." Lenore picked up one of her brushes.

"The damage is done! Everyone will know that he took part in our picnic. Even if Mr. Ramsdell should remove himself to the Orient, your names will be bandied about."

"Nonsense. Dear friend, but you are annoying at times!"

Belinda lowered her voice so that the servants couldn't hear her. "You invited him to join us because you are in love with him."

"Fiddlesticks. You know me better than that. I did not invite him."

"He fascinates you, Lenore. He is forbidden fruit, and all the more attractive for it."

"I am losing all patience with you, Belinda." Lenore's spirits sank lower with every word, because she suspected Belinda's statements held some truth. *But I am in control of my feelings. Eric means nothing to me,* Lenore thought defensively.

"Lenore, you are more than you know to Mr. Ramsdell. But you don't seem to mind it. He could easily be in control of your feelings, and you would sigh every day when he's not with you." Her voice rose with outrage on the last words.

Lenore remained silent. If she began to argue, she might lose her friend along the way.

"If you are that desperate, find a gentleman with whom you can flirt without putting everyone's nose out of joint in the process. I don't want to watch you make a fool out of yourself. As Edward says, the Marquess of Ludbank is an excellent catch."

"I am well aware of that. But I don't want to marry him. I would rather find myself a young lover, perhaps an artist."

"Pooh, you want Mr. Ramsdell as a lover. Obviously, he's attracted to you as well. But I know he will love you and leave you, enjoy whatever affection he can from you as you long for his embrace. And furthermore, he'll leave your reputation in total ruin. A true gentleman like, say, Ludbank, protects your good name."

"He bores me no end."

"Then you need a highwayman or some other unattainable hero figure."

"You read too many melodramatic novels, Belinda." Lenore started laughing. "Listen to us! Two old biddies desperately discussing possible romantic prospects."

Belinda's eyes filled with tears. "I . . . well, I don't know what to say—I've never told you this, but I have a young lover, an artist who wants everything from me except my heart."

Lenore looked at her in shock. "What—?"

"You heard every word. I had a great need to find out what it's like to be loved properly. As you know Adam only does his duty, without a trace of delight. Leopold taught me about passion, but he has no heart." She started crying without making a sound, and Lenore felt her pain.

Lenore placed her hand on her friend's arm. "I didn't know you were suffering thus. You haven't said a word."

Belinda dried her eyes on a handkerchief. "It isn't something that's easy to talk about."

"Where is he now?"

"In London still. I can't break off with him even if I so desire. It's as if he has cast a spell on me."

"You're strong enough to break away, Belinda."

"When I try, I grow desperate after a few days and write to him." She gave Lenore a pleading look. "I don't want you to fall into that trap. Mr. Ramsdell has so much experience—"

"I have no desire to start a romantic dalliance with Mr. Ramsdell!"

"Don't you see?" Belinda's voice took on a high-pitched note. "It's already happening! Next you shall surrender in his arms. It's been so long since your marriage bed, and one longs for . . . things."

Lenore felt defensive. "Well—"

"Mr. Ramsdell is an expert," Belinda said with deep agitation. "He will seduce you so smoothly that you won't know what happened, and then he'll discard you just as smoothly."

Lenore didn't know how to reply. "It will never go that far," she said.

"The gentlemen will be placing wagers at the clubs. The extra spice to the story is that Ramsdell is supposed to be your enemy. You'll be the topic of all the letters traveling between the country estates, and Edward will banish you forever."

"Oh, stuff and nonsense," Lenore chided, perturbed.

"I know they'll be betting heavily at the clubs tonight, and you'll find that whoever is left in London will snub you."

"That is pure fustian. I have done nothing."

"Ramsdell did not visit here to be polite. He has nefarious schemes to nurture."

"You're much too grim, Belinda." Yet her words made Lenore cringe. What if she was right? What if his only motive was to ruin her? He must be very angry about the accusations around Cedric's death, whether he was guilty or not.

"He was riling you only to get closer to you; he aimed to tear down your barriers. Not that it's that difficult."

"He spoke about how to be a good listener and a good mate. It was strange; he could have taken the words right out of my mind. Everything I've ever claimed—from my own experience—he put into his own words."

"I hope you don't believe a word of his." Belinda wrapped her arms around her middle as if cold.

Lenore had never felt more confused. "I don't know what to believe. He sounded very convincing, almost pleading with me to give him a chance to show his sincerity."

"Again, are you going to swallow that twaddle? You give everyone the benefit of the doubt, yet you champion the wrong people as if you had a strange desire to get burned."

Lenore flung one of her brushes onto the grass. "I do not! If anything, I'll never be taken advantage of again."

"You're vulnerable and you don't see it."

Lenore couldn't argue the point. "This started out as a wonderful morning. I so enjoy coming to the park to paint, but we've entered a nightmare. How will I ever know the truth?"

"Stand by your principles and don't allow yourself to be taken in by Mr. Ramsdell's blandishments."

Belinda's words made sense, but there was a bleakness to the situation that no common sense advice could erase.

"I think it's time to go home."

The next day Charlie paid Lenore a visit. "I am at my wits' end," he complained and raked a hand through his carefully arranged hair, wreaking havoc to his curls. "In good faith, I invited old Ricky to spend time with me here in London, and now he's making eyes at my fairest Davina. The outrageous part is that she's making eyes back. He had a bit of an accident, fell out of the saddle as his mount reared at an aggressive dog. High-strung animal and not fit for London parks, don't you know."

Lenore nodded, her eyes gritty from lack of sleep.

"Well, the horse reared right next to fair Davina's carriage, and as Ricky bumped his head, they all—Davina, her aunt and cousin, and a friend—urged him to lie down in the barouche. Then they fussed over him and dabbed his temples with rose water." Charlie's voice filled with despair. "I was nauseated to hear about it. All that time, fair Davina held his hand and smiled at him reassuringly. I was mortified. The cruelty of that . . . that *creature!*"

"You cannot help what you feel, Charlie, and neither can she. By the sound of it, she has no tender feelings for you. I hate to be that cruel, but the truth is always best in the long run."

"Yes, rub it in with acid," he muttered to the floor, his head in his hands. His voice sounded muffled, as if he were crying.

"Oh, Charlie."

"Don't—" His voice broke off.

It made Lenore uncomfortable to witness his misery. This could be her if she gave in to her feelings for Eric Ramsdell. She had admitted to herself in the dark hours of the early morning when she lay sleepless and tossing that she had developed a wild *tendre* for Eric Ramsdell.

"What should I do, Lenore?"

"You must forget the fair Davina. She is unworthy of your affection. Everyone knows she likes to play favorites, and I daresay Ricky will be nothing more than a memory come Christmas."

"I will not survive that long. A sickness, a longing of

such depth has entered my being, and I'm slowly being consumed. I shall fade away and die."

"Most people survive unrequited love, Charlie. If you don't see her for a while, she'll leave your mind."

"Ricky proudly announced that she invited him to join her in her box at the theater tonight. He's walking on clouds, and the lump on his head is actually a gift if you listen to him going on. Nauseating. I had to get out of the house."

"I can understand that."

He sniveled and slowly pulled himself together. "Do you want to go with me to the theater?"

"So that you can torture yourself by staring at *her*? I think not!"

He studied her with bloodshot eyes and waved his hands helplessly. "Be gentle with me, Lenore, I beg of you."

"Oh, that word again," she muttered to herself.

"I beg your pardon?"

"Nothing, Charlie. The word 'gentle.'"

"What is it that I hear about you, Lenore? You made a spectacle of yourself in the park with Eric yesterday?"

"So the rumors are already flying." Belinda had been right on that score. "Remember, Charlie, you introduced me to Eric Ramsdell."

"Yes, I wanted to poke my left eye out with a stick when I remembered his connection to Cedric. It had completely flown out of my mind."

"You are rather forgetful, so I know you're speaking the truth. I forgive you."

He clasped her hand between his two pudgy ones. "Thank you, fair friend. But what is it that I hear about you? Tell me it's not true."

"Are the gentlemen placing bets on the outcome of my, er, battle with Eric Ramsdell?"

"Battle?" Charlie's eyes grew round. "Why would you do battle with him?"

Lenore squirmed on the hard settee in the foyer. Charlie had not advanced further than there before he blurted out his torment. She answered softly. "We, well, we aren't exactly battling, but I have talked to him, and gossipmongers saw us in the park."

"Edward will be furious."

"He is always furious with me. It makes no difference."

"You have a point."

She felt disheveled and noticed the wrinkles on her rose sarcenet gown. She knew her hair looked a fright, but Charlie didn't seem to mind.

"As far as I know, nothing has happened in the club to indicate your disgrace. No bets."

Lenore sighed with relief. Perhaps nothing would come of this, and she promised herself she would never speak to Eric again. She had been utterly foolish yesterday. But Eric's presence had pushed her too far, and there had been something about the sparks flying between them that had befuddled her mind.

Perhaps she should take a young lover. She glanced at Charlie knowing he would be shocked if he could read her thoughts. He would rather see her within the safety of marriage. "Are you ever going to marry, Charlie?"

"Leg-shackled? Me? Only if it's to the fair Davina. Anyone else won't do," he said gloomily.

"And what if she ends up marrying someone else?"

"Then I shall wither away with grief." He pushed his hands through his hair anew, putting his curls in further disarray. His voice became a lament. "Why are you torturing me with such questions?"

"I'm just being honest."

He took her hands and held them tight. His blue eyes pleaded with her. "Will you help me? Please, please help me."

Lenore cast about in her mind for clues. "How?"

"You know Davina, even if you're not terribly close. She leaves London next week, and I'm desperate to spend some time alone with her. That will give me a chance to show my sterling qualities."

She had a sinking feeling in her stomach, and she worried about her friend's emotional health. "I don't know . . ."

"You have to help me, Lenore." He sounded so desperate her heart filled with compassion. And Eric had accused her of having none!

"Yes . . . well, I'll try to help you, Charlie. Shall I invite Davina and her chaperone to a small dinner party, or what do you prefer?"

"Oh no, her chaperone is a hawk. She won't let us alone for a minute. We'll have to try Vauxhall Gardens where desperate lovers can disappear—and not be found for a few minutes."

"I see no reason to offer invitations to Vauxhall. Actually it would be distasteful to take such a step."

"Persuade Ludbank to help you. He could invite a party to the Vauxhall fireworks. Davina won't refuse a man of such influence."

"I am trying to avoid Ludbank."

"You can't do that, Lenore. He's your salvation." Charlie squeezed her hands harder.

"Don't be ridiculous, Charlie!" She pulled her hands back and started pacing the foyer. In a silver urn stood a bunch of pink phlox and veronica, and she tweaked off a wayward green leaf.

"You seem upset, Lenore. What has happened? Don't tell me you gave Ludbank his congé. Not a good idea."

"Of course I haven't. Ludbank is not on my mind these days. I haven't seen him lately, or heard from him."

"Very foolish of you. Ladies are standing in line to lead him down the aisle. You are too obstinate for your own good."

"Everyone is berating me at every turn. All I have done is lead my own life and I hear nothing but complaints about the way I'm doing it. Have I hurt anyone?"

He shook his head. "Not that I know. People are just astounded by your choices. You are too independent, m'dear."

"I take that as a compliment, Charlie."

He looked miserable. "I need to know where I stand with the fair Davina—if there's the slightest chance of true bliss."

"You're doing it too brown," Lenore scoffed, exasperated with her friend, whose weakness made her uncomfortable. "Put your nose in the air as she passes you on the street, and she might pay you some attention. Love to her is a game. And if you seem too eager, the game is over."

He looked at her incredulously. "Are you telling me to be rude?"

"Not a wholly bad idea," she said. "Pretend that every woman is more interesting than she, and it's bound to have an effect. She cannot bear not being the center of attention."

"A most unkind observation."

Lenore shrugged. "If you want her attention, you'll have to ignore her."

"What if the whole thing fails?"

"As it is, you are getting nowhere. Ricky is halfway down the aisle with her."

His sigh was heavier than his portly bulk, and his hands dangled helplessly between his legs. "I do hope you're right, Lenore. If not, I shall kill myself."

"Don't be ridiculous! I'm quite out of patience with you."

"You'll get Ludbank to help you?"

She nodded. "I shall hint that I'd like an evening at Vauxhall to listen to the music."

"Then I can lure Davina—"

"No! You are to act indifferent. Let her lure you down a dark path."

"That would never happen."

"Probably not, seeing as she's always guarded by that dragon of a chaperone, but mayhap she can contrive to escape for one moment."

"She will be wed before the next Season, I'm sure," he said, his voice still gloomy. "I couldn't stand the possibility that she'd marry some greenhorn like Ricky."

"You see only beauty in her, but I know she's both spoiled and immature. If she falls in love with that greenhorn, it only proves that I'm right. You would be much happier with someone else."

"What about you, Lenore? You sound so disillusioned. But you are beautiful and compassionate. Ludbank should consider himself fortunate that you would even deign to acknowledge his advances."

Lenore laughed. "You're lifting my spirits, Charlie. I've felt very low lately."

"Not as blue-deviled as I, surely."

"Probably not; I've not reached that level of desperation, and I won't. I won't allow myself."

Charlie heaved another sigh. "Oh, Lenore, I can't sleep a wink until I have her in my arms."

"You nincompoop. She'll complain about your snoring, and if not that, it'll be something else."

"You certainly know how to prick my bubble of hope."

"Because her sterling qualities are only in your imagination."

"You sound so sure of that, Lenore."

"Mark my words, Davina will always expect to be treated like royalty. I suspect you would tire of her quickly."

"Never!"

Lenore sighed. "It is only a silly infatuation, Charlie."

"Now you're cruel to boot."

"Count on a visit to Vauxhall on Saturday night. I shall prove my point to you."

Chapter 13

Eric read the last entry in the journal, and discovered that he had repeated some of Lenore's expressions almost verbatim when he spoke with her at the picnic. No wonder she had said it sounded familiar. *You clothhead,* he berated himself and was grateful that she hadn't connected their conversation to her diary.

He lifted his goose quill and dipped it in the inkhorn. She was right, of course, and he didn't really have anything to say, but he had to reply.

> *Your entry was full of wisdom, and I feel you hit your mark when you pointed out the facts of my current situation. Having met the lady who has ignited my heart, I sorely need to learn the intricacies of a true courtship. You speak of finding the essence of love—I am at a loss there—but I agree that a loving heart brings happiness.*
>
> *My dog, Clarence, taught me as much as I grew up. We were inseparable companions and he loved me with selfless adoration. We were boundlessly happy together. I was heartbroken when he died of old age.*
>
> *I also had a cat I could never please. Only when I neglected her would she deign to pay me attention. I can almost hear you scoff at my pitiful stories, but I surmise*

*the principle stands for love. The females of my ac-
quaintance are as fickle as cats, without the fidelity of
dogs and would willfully act upon their own schemes.
However, none ever touched my heart, so I didn't care,
and that infuriated them.*

*Love is above all a teacher, either a lenient one or a
stern one, depending on one's inclination. I agree with
you also, that real love requires honesty. I also realize I
lack humility, something that doesn't come easily.*

He rubbed his aching eyes as he put down the quill.
How that love ached in his heart, and here he was trying to reach out, but his quill put only theories onto
paper. To actually experience love with someone who
would never trust him—no, that was impossible.

But if he could find a way to prove to Lenore that
he was an excellent student and a quick study. . . .

Sir Winton would never cooperate, and Lenore
would never believe his innocence. Even if she said
she did, the question surrounding Cedric's death
would always come between them. He blotted the wet
ink and decided to have the diary delivered to the
Rose Tearoom and not to her home. By now, she
probably had spies posted to catch him; if she discovered his identity, she would never speak with him
again.

Saturday came, and Charlie visited him in the morning, sharing a breakfast of kippers, bacon, and eggs.

"You look rather the worse for wear, Charlie. Did
you stare too deeply into the bottle last night?"

His friend stared at his untouched plate of food. "I

did not drink a drop, nor did I eat. I'm becoming a shadow of myself."

"You cannot pine away forever! Have you no pride?" Eric arranged kippers on a piece of toast and took a bite.

"You don't know what it's like."

"I might, y'know. I, however, take care to avoid the 'illness' you're experiencing. True love will never get that sort of grip on me."

Charlie gave him a look full of pain. "That's prudent, my friend." He poked the eggs with his fork. "I hear you encountered Lenore in the park, and that you picnicked together. The town is buzzing with gossip."

"Mrs. Chandler was there also. We met in broad daylight in public. Not exactly an illict tryst."

"Denbury has been wandering about in a fit of rage for days and won't speak to her. I wouldn't be surprised if he seeks satisfaction from you."

"But I didn't do anything. Lenore and I had a polite conversation for half an hour, and I drank a glass of sherry with her."

"She'll never survive the gossip. Why she even considered talking to you is a mystery to me. You're conspiring to ruin her."

"Not at all . . . but I realize it looks suspect." Eric took a deep breath and set down the remnants of his toast. "I have to confess something to you. But if you speak of it, I shall call you out, and let me remind you that you're a terrible shot."

"What's so dire?" Charlie asked, his expression startled.

"I am in love with Lenore Andrews."

Silence fell like a hammer blow in the room. "What—?" Charlie gasped.

"I've fallen in love. I never thought that would happen. In other words, you and I are in the same boat—in love with women we can't have."

Charlie sighed and gulped down some coffee. "Thunder and turf, Eric. What are we going to do?"

"I don't know. I can't see a way to approach Lenore now. The gossip must have affected her, and she has to protect herself."

"That's not the only reason. I highly doubt she *wants* to see you."

"According to her, she doesn't care about convention."

"Yes, but she has to think of her family. She would never consider destroying Edward by her amorous choices. She's too proud for that."

Eric nodded. "You're right on that score."

"I saw Edward last night and he is furious. I would stay inside if I were you, or find your cheek slapped."

Eric laughed. "I shall not hide. I'm man enough to face his ire, and I don't regret my meeting with Lenore."

"I'm not surprised that you're taken with her, but under the circumstances . . . and Edward is pushing her to accept Ludbank's proposal."

"Has he offered for her?"

"He hasn't approached her directly—I suppose he's aware of her reluctance—but he's cleared his intentions with Edward. It's only a matter of time."

"I see." He paused. "Lenore doesn't love him."

"You believe she loves you?"

Eric pondered the question, but he had no real answer. "I don't know. If circumstances were different . . ."

"You'll have to discover her true feelings somehow. I know, we're going to Vauxhall tonight—Ludbank has contrived to invite the fair Davina, and Ricky is not attending. I'll have my chance to captivate her tonight."

"That's interesting. I hope you make some progress, or that she disillusions you so thoroughly that you'll be disgusted with her."

"Don't say things like that, Eric!" Charlie wailed.

"You would find it a blessing, I'm sure—you being cured of the illness. It would be like waking up from a nightmare."

"Nonsense! You just don't know what it's like to truly be in love."

"Unrequited love that is. Obsession."

Charlie threw him a dark glance. "I'm annoyed with you, but you're welcome to appear at the gathering at Vauxhall. I don't know what will occur. Ludbank might call you out, but Lenore might choose to have a secret tryst with you in the park. You never know with her." He scratched his chin under the tight neck cloth. "Rightfully, I should side with her and not you. In fact, I should not be sharing breakfast with you this morning, but you are my friend. It's a most awkward situation."

"Don't worry. You're safe from any harm—"

"Unless Ludbank finds out I invited you to appear at Vauxhall."

"He'll never discover the truth from me, and I'd be the only one who knows." He gave Eric a shrewd glance. "Just another adventure for you. As I recall, you thrive on adventure."

Eric could not argue, but he longed for more than that. "Anything I can do to further your hopes with the fair Davina?"

"Just stay away from her, you handsome devil!"

Eric laughed. "She won't even know I am there."

"I'll contrive a meeting between you and Lenore at half past ten. Meet us at the fountain. I'll make up an excuse for her to join me."

The evening was balmy, yet a damp wind from the sea promised rain across the city. Eric looked toward the sky as he stepped out of the Blythe mansion. Clouds hung heavy in the darkness, obscuring any stars. Uneasiness had taken hold of him, and he wondered about the wisdom of attending Vauxhall.

Still, nothing could have kept him away.

At ten o'clock velvet darkness hung over the park, and the lanterns swung in the light wind. The Grotto looked as inviting as it always did, and patrons dotted the area, the dinner tables full. Glasses chinked, and laughter filled the air.

He'd never felt more outside the circle of warm friendship as the guests enjoyed their night together. He spotted Charlie by his garish green coat in one of the far booths, and then he noticed Ludbank, the lion basking in the glory of everyone's admiration.

Eric leaned against a Grecian pillar behind a potted palm and stared at the scene. Lenore sat next to Ludbank, her dark hair up in masses of curls. Her teeth gleamed every time she smiled, and her creamy shoulders peeked out from under a shimmering fringed Indian shawl. He'd never seen her look more beautiful, and his heart twisted in his chest. Unattainable at best, he thought.

He shifted on his feet, and experienced a wave of frustration. If only he could join the party and gaze into her dark eyes.

Charlie sat across the table from the fair Davina,

and Eric noticed that the man acted strangely. Instead of hanging on her every movement, he seemed to be ignoring her completely. When someone paid her a compliment and she simpered, her fan fluttering, he paid no heed.

What had brought on this turnaround? Charlie had been dying for a glance from her cruel blue eyes.

Eric took a walk down one of the sparsely lit paths. In ten minutes he would stand face-to-face with Lenore, and he had no idea what he would say. He wondered if someone had picked up the journal at the tearoom and if she'd read his entry, but it didn't matter at this point. A glance spoke volumes, not painstaking words.

When he returned, she was there at the fountain with Charlie, just as he had promised. Eric hesitated. What if she refused to speak with him? He would have to take his chances. He braced his shoulders and stepped out of the shadows. She saw him at once and flinched visibly. He bowed.

"How is your ankle, Lenore? I see that you're walking again."

"Yes." Her voice faltered with hesitation. "I still have some pain and a limp, but I'm almost restored to full health."

"I'm delighted to hear it."

She looked around as if expecting everyone who had gossiped about her behavior in the park to appear and berate her, but no one arrived. The three of them stood awkwardly at the fountain, the crystal tinkling of the water the only sound.

"What are you doing here?" she asked at last as her gaze darted from him to Charlie.

Charlie looked uncomfortable. "It was your idea, wasn't it?" she asked her friend. "You whispered that you desperately needed advice in private, and I assumed it was about Davina. Fool that I am."

"Lenore, it isn't like that." Charlie wrung his hands. "You are both my friends, and I want you to give Eric a chance. I believe wholeheartedly in his innocence. He doesn't have it in him to kill anyone."

Lenore looked at Eric uncertainly. "It still doesn't change the fact that we're having a clandestine meeting in the gardens."

"'Tis not clandestine!" Charlie blurted out. "You're here with me—an old bosom bow and protector."

Lenore couldn't help but laugh at the expression. "Of all the ridiculous—"

"Before you two have a coze, are my tactics to entice the fair Davina working?" he asked, breathless now as emotion was taking over. "Say that they are, Lenore!"

"She looked at you speculatively a few times, probably wondering why you weren't basking in her light tonight. Just wait and see what happens."

He looked supremely uncomfortable. "Where do I find the strength? I'm about ready to explode."

She laughed. "Consider it as the greatest trial of your life—so far." She gave him a hard stare. "I foresee the trials continuing should you succeed in this. Miss Davina Bright would not be easy to please. She would run you ragged as you hastened to gratify her every whim. Still, she wouldn't be satisfied."

"You are quite wrong. She's an angel and no mistake about it."

Lenore didn't reply to that. His obliviousness clearly worried her, and Eric hoped that Charlie would have a taste of Davina's cruel selfishness before it was too late.

"I shall contrive to look bored with her for the rest of the evening." Charlie sank down on a bench by the fountain, his demeanor dejected. Lenore stared uneasily at Eric, and he wondered if she would venture on a walk with him.

"Will you take some air with me?" he asked.

"Only for a few minutes, mind you," Charlie continued. "We have to return to the table, or Ludbank will wonder what happened to Lenore."

"Why do you surmise I'd like to walk, or even speak with you, Eric?" She took a step backward, but he followed and gently gripped her arm.

"Come, Lenore," he whispered. "I worry about Charlie." He pulled her with him onto one of the paths, and she didn't protest, which elated him.

"Seems we have wandered this path before," she said and stopped, right under a lantern. "I'm not going any further."

"Very well, but aren't you concerned about Charlie?"

"Of course I am," she said with a tinge of anger. "He's sadly addlepated, and I'm quite out of patience with him. I feel as if I have to watch his every step lest he trip himself."

"Love makes a fool of us all."

She fell silent, and he wished he could read her thoughts. He pulled her hand through his arm, the warmth of her skin igniting the warmth in his heart. "I suspect you've received rakedowns for the picnick in the park, but I suppose you knew what was coming."

She nodded. "The sherry went to my head, but I honestly don't care what other people think about me."

"You'll end up as this generation's black sheep of the Brigham family."

Her laugh bubbled up like a sparkling brook in

spring. He had no idea from where these poetic expressions in his mind originated. He had never been prone to poetry with females, except with Lenore.

"If Ludbank finds us here, he'll call you out." She looked toward the fountain, but only Charlie sat on the bench, his head hanging.

"I'm not worried," he said and slowly pulled her closer. "I'm a great shot and a bruiser with swords."

"I don't want any bloodshed on my conscience. I'd rather pull back than antagonize people who are close to me. My brother would run you through right here without the courtesy of seconds."

"I didn't bring my sword. However, if you were the last treasure my eyes focused on in my last moment, I could leave this world content."

"Why?" She looked puzzled.

"Because you've sparked feelings in me that I've never felt before. That's a great gift, and a great feat on your part."

"What kind of feelings?"

He pulled her ever closer until he could feel the contours of her body touching his. "I think it may be . . . eh, love?"

"Love?" She laughed incredulously. "Don't be absurd."

Deflated, he stiffened. "What's absurd about it?"

"You don't know me well enough to love me, and I am not sure you are capable of any tender feelings. You and Miss Bright are cut from the same cloth— always thinking of yourselves first."

His breath caught in his throat. "That's a rather cruel thing to say, Lenore, and I don't deserve it. You're playing a game now. If you so adamantly believe the rumors about my character, you would run away, screaming. But you seem just as intrigued with me as I am with you."

"Utter bunkum, I say."

"You can say anything you like, but action speaks louder than words."

"Piffle."

He cupped her neck with his hands as a delicious shiver went down his spine. Without another word, he pulled her to him and kissed her warm mouth. Nothing had ever tasted sweeter to him. Inspired, he held her even closer and kissed her so thoroughly she seemed to lose her balance.

Only when shouts came from the path behind them, did he pull away, his head dizzy and his body on fire. Vaguely did he hear his name, and through the daze, he recognized Charlie's worried tones. "Not that way, Ludbank. She went in the opposite direction."

Lenore didn't appear to have heard a word, and he pushed her limp body behind him. Only then did she come around and cling to his arm. Two men were marching down the path, and Eric recognized Ludbank's imposing figure, and behind him, Lord Denbury, Lenore's brother. He braced himself to face their inevitable wrath.

Ludbank stood in front of him, his face a mask of fury. "Name your seconds, sirrah," he shouted and slapped Eric on the cheek with his glove.

Before Eric could open his mouth, Denbury slapped him on the other cheek and demanded that he name his seconds.

Lenore gasped behind Eric and cringed as Denbury slapped him.

"Edward! What are you doing?"

"Defending your honor since you can't seem to stay

out of harm's way. I am also defending the family honor."

"I demand satisfaction! You have dishonored the woman I intend to marry," Ludbank shouted for all to hear.

"That's balderdash," Lenore said. "I've never promised to wed you, Ludbank, and I won't now. I might've toyed with the idea at one time, but I cannot abide your autocratic behavior and your temper. You might as well call me out too." She stepped forward, her whole stance challenging him.

"Don't be ridiculous, Lenore," Ludbank said, pulling her aside. "My quarrel is not with you, but after tonight, I don't know how your reputation stands in the world. I don't want to be pulled into scandal because of your wanton behavior."

"We were just talking," she said lamely.

"Don't lie. It was clear as day that he was *kissing* you." His voice rose on the last words, and she took a step back, bumping against Eric.

He steadied her arm. "Lenore, go to the fountain and find Charlie. He'll take care of you."

She looked incredulous. "And leave you to face these mad dogs alone?"

He couldn't help but laugh. "Just an evening's work."

"I won't be able to sleep a wink with this hanging over me," she said as she stepped away.

"You should've thought about that before you walked down this path," Denbury shouted. "Go back to your table."

Eric saw mutiny in her eyes, but he motioned to her to leave. She started to say something, then obeyed. He could sense her heart going out to him, and that strengthened him as a flash of insight made it clear he hadn't done anything wrong. He hadn't forced her at all, and she had responded with passion.

"Gentlemen, let us set up a time and a meeting place," he said briskly, as the two gentlemen evidently wanted to dispatch him then and there. "Pistols, of course."

"Barn Elms at dawn, two days hence," Denbury said.

"I was first," Ludbank said in hurt tones.

"I'll go after you then." The tension in Denbury's voice made things worse.

"That is, if there's anything left of him," Ludbank said. His lofty tones must rub Denbury the wrong way, Eric thought.

"Perhaps we could find a peaceful solution. Duels are illegal, after all." Eric had no desire to get up that early and face these two hotheads first thing in the morning. He would hardly have time to drink his coffee that early.

"Peaceful? When you wreak havoc with my family?" Denbury bristled, practically spitting the words out.

"And you've seriously overstepped your territory— onto mine," Ludbank said.

Eric folded his arms over his chest. "That's nonsense. I haven't heard Lenore give her consent to a union with you."

"She will in due time."

"I believe you're sorely misreading her intentions."

Denbury broke in. "If you think you can wangle a way into our family with your scandalous reputation, you're sadly deluded. If I ever see you speaking to my sister again, I shall shoot you without warning."

Eric was quite out of patience with the men. "Nonsense."

"Or I will," Ludbank said. "If you're still alive!"

"Shooting me would put a chink in your righteous armor, Denbury. The scandal that would cause would close all the doors to the establishments."

"We would be in the same boat then. You can have a taste of what Cedric endured at your hand."

"Cedric, I believe, never had to endure a thing. He did as he pleased, and I'm quite certain he was killed with a drunken smile on his lips and a brandy bottle in his hand."

Denbury loomed closer. "How do you know that?"

"I knew Cedric's character. You would rarely see him abroad without a bottle and ready for any kind of prank. He would have died as he lived, carelessly."

There wasn't much Denbury could reply to that, but Eric understood that the issue was far from closed. Clearly, Denbury longed to put a bullet through his heart to avenge his brother's death. It didn't matter who was guilty.

"I'm certain you are eager, but you must wait two days," Eric said. "And you know my reputation in marksmanship."

"Don't brag so!" Denbury cried. "How dare you!"

"Blast and damn," Eric said, "we're acting like a group of young hotheads."

They mumbled something at that, and suddenly Denbury turned around and marched off. "Two days hence," he bellowed over his shoulder.

"Why doesn't he let the whole world know, and Bow Street as well?" Eric said.

"Well, you're not very popular at Bow Street, so I would pray they are not notified," Ludbank said. "How could you come to Vauxhall and lure my almost fiancée down this dark path? Your intentions were far from noble."

Eric didn't reply. He suspected that if he said anything, Ludbank would take that out on Lenore. He wanted to protect her at all costs, which was also a new kind of feeling for him, and he liked it.

"Make the best of the two days you have left to live," Ludbank said and stomped down the sandy path.

Chapter 14

Lenore, her emotions in a wild tangle, went back to the table with Charlie, who apologized the whole way. So caught up in his own dreams, he'd neglected his duty as a sentinel. "I can't tear my thoughts away from the fair Davina. Are you sure I'm acting the right way? What if she rejects me most cruelly?"

"It's the only way to treat her," Lenore answered, annoyed at his insecurity. "Make yourself unreachable."

"I don't see the point," Charlie said in a low, trembling voice, and Lenore elbowed him in the side.

They reached the table, and Davina's chaperone, Mrs. Millspoon, leaned sideways to see them better. "Is everything in order? It's highly irregular for Sir Charles to ask you aside—alone."

Lenore laughed. "Don't worry. I've known Charlie practically all my life."

Mrs. Millspoon turned up her nose. "I'm sure."

As they sat down, Charlie struggled to maintain his bored and distant expression, and he avoided Davina's darting glances. Lenore sensed her curiosity. Stretching forward, Lenore whispered in her ear, "Sir Charles is deluged with the attention of admiring ladies, and he had to ask my advice on how to stay clear of them.

He wouldn't want to find himself in a compromising situation with an amorous female."

Davina's eyes grew round, her sweep of eyelashes curling beguilingly. "Is he that popular? I thought him rather a bore with his constant hangdog expression," she whispered back.

"You're mistaken. He has everyone at his beck and call. There was a lady who practically threw herself in front of his carriage to get his attention."

"Really?" The blue angelic eyes grew even rounder. "What was her name?"

"I don't rightly know and I wouldn't want to spread gossip. Anyhow, she didn't sustain any injuries, and she had no luck with Charlie."

Davina fluttered her fan and stared at Charlie speculatively. "I'm shocked beyond belief," she said.

Lenore could tell that the idea of Charlie's popularity intrigued her, but Lenore wasn't going to tell her it had been a flower seller who had tripped on a broom and fallen near the coach. "Anyone would consider herself fortunate to have Charlie's attention."

Charlie was tapping his fingertips on the table, improving on his expression of ennui. He gave his fingernails a bored study.

"He can't be that popular; you must be joking," Davina said.

Lenore shook her head. "No."

"Perhaps I should talk to him? Or would it be a waste of time? He might be more interesting than I thought, but he has no style. He'll have to talk about things that interest me, though. Masculine pastimes do not interest me."

"Fashion, flower arrangements?"

"Oh no, I *never* arrange flowers," she said, looking shocked. "That's for the servants to do."

"I see. Well, you've missed a calming and useful endeavor."

"*I* wouldn't want to get *my* hands soiled and my fingertips pricked with thorns," Davina said with emphasis.

Lenore could not reply to that, and didn't want to as she might say something that might ruin everything. She winked at Charlie, whose eyes widened a fraction.

Davina leaned forward, staring hard at Charlie at the opposite side of the table. "I daresay you invest in only the finest tailors, Sir Charles? Others are sadly lacking in style, don't you agree?"

Charlie almost fell off his chair, Lenore noticed, and she felt a sense of accomplishment as she'd managed to connect the two at last. Charlie was now forever in her debt.

She lapsed into the memory of Eric's knee-melting kiss and wondered how she could be so wanton as to allow these things to happen, one time after the other. She had completely lost her senses, and now her brother was going to shoot the man through the heart! Fear washed through her, an icy wave she couldn't stem.

Why was this happening?

Was there anything she could do to stop them? Denbury would do his best to kill Eric, the man who had ignited her passion, an emotion she thought had been dead since she discovered Ronald's duplicity.

If only she could talk some sense into these men, set on battle as they were.

She looked up and there they were, Ludbank and Denbury. They sat down on each side of her, as if to close her in and make sure she didn't leave again.

Maria Greene

"You're completely beyond the pale now," Denbury hissed from the side of his mouth. "I shall ship you to the spinster aunts posthaste. This has gone too far, and you've proved yourself to be silly and unreliable. 'Tis fortunate that no one else saw you on the path or this latest scandal would be all over London by now."

"And then I could certainly not marry you," Ludbank said into her other ear. "I don't need a scandal attached to my name."

She wanted to scream, but she only smiled politely and gave him a lethal look. She wished the evening were over, but Charlie was busily discussing Belgian laces and the latest fashions from Paris with Davina Bright. She had no idea where he got all the information, unless he made everything up. But Davina would know the truth.

"I think we should leave. This evening has been a grave disappointment," Ludbank said.

"Indeed," Denbury said, and looked imperatively at Lenore. "Shall we take our leave?"

"I'm not going with you, Edward. Charlie or Ludbank can bring me home. Please remember that I am of age, and you cannot order me about." She placed her hand on his arm. "If you stoop so low as to meet Mr. Ramsdell for a duel at dawn, I shan't speak to you again."

He bared his teeth. "Justice did not work in our favor when Cedric died. Ramsdell was cleared because Lord Blythe knows every judge in town. Sometimes you have to take justice into your own hands."

"Not unless you're absolutely sure your judgment is correct," she replied icily.

Edward looked as if he could explode at any moment. "You're acting like a complete thimblewit,

Lenore. Of course he's guilty! No one else was there to pull the trigger."

"He claims someone was, but he can't prove it."

"And you choose to believe such balderdash? It's the outside of enough, and I'm quite weary of the whole business—and you." He nodded curtly and left the table without a word of farewell.

Edward was in high dudgeon, she thought with a sigh. Her brother was like a bull that doesn't want to look left or right. She turned toward Ludbank, who didn't appear to be in any better frame of mind. His mouth was compressed to a grim line, his forehead furrowed.

"What do you think, Ludbank? Do you have an original thought, or do you only follow my brother's lead?" She knew the impertinent questions would anger him, but she couldn't stop herself. The whole world had gone mad.

"I knew someone named Lilly once, a lovely girl," he said. "She was quite keen on me."

"Mayhap you ought to find out if she's still unwed," Lenore suggested, feeling quite ruthless.

He looked at her with his handsome brown eyes. "I thought we had an understanding."

"That might be what *you* thought. Somehow you neglected to tell me."

"I don't see how you could possibly reject me."

The gall of the man.

"I find it easy." These self-absorbed people exhausted her, Davina included. Now *she* and Ludbank would be a perfect match. Their breakfast conversation would be totally at cross-purposes, but neither of them would notice.

She glanced at the woman in question, who was now

asking Charlie's opinion about two different kinds of velvet. Charlie hung on her every word like a dog. Lenore wanted to sigh at his foolishness. Love was a game of illusion, she thought, Cupid a dashed trickster!

"I am surprised your attention hasn't wandered to the fair Davina, Ludbank. After all, she's the catch of the Season, and you're very eligible." Her gaze went from one to the other. "Hmm, you would make a rather handsome couple."

Ludbank scowled, clearly annoyed with her indifference. After all, he wasn't used to rejection. "She's too young for me, though I find her lovely as most do." He looked more closely at Lenore, and she stifled the urge to leave. "I daresay it's time I make my intentions clear to you. I hadn't planned on approaching you on an occasion like this, but I might as well." He held out his arm to her. "Would you mind strolling in the park with me?"

She avoided his gesture. "Yes, I'd mind! Desist with this foolery, Ludbank! You know my feelings—or lack thereof. I don't want to hurt your feelings further."

He straightened his back, his chin jutting out aggressively. "I see."

"I don't know if you do, Ludbank."

"Don't be ridiculous, Lenore."

She raised her eyebrows, her gaze challenging him. "Well, are we in accord?"

He looked somewhat pale, she thought.

"Yes, I daresay we are. At least you didn't let me make a fool of myself at your feet."

"Now that the matter is resolved, what about the duel? Are you still going to fight Mr. Ramsdell?"

"Absolutely. The man has no conscience, and even

if I don't have a personal stake to protect, I care about your safety."

"Your anger has overtaken your reason."

He pursed his lips, displeasure evident in every line of his face. "You don't understand the code of honor. This is the business of gentlemen, and I don't expect you to know anything about it. I am protecting *your* honor, and yet you're determined to throw it all away."

Quite exasperated, Lenore thought again, that it was a silly tradition to rush into the mouth of a roaring lion, all in the name of honor. Ladies would never do anything so idiotic. "I wouldn't want to offend you," she said noncommittally. "Yet, I don't believe in violence, and both of you—"

"Code of honor!" he said sternly.

She gave up. It was time to leave. The evening had exhausted her.

She tried to catch Charlie's eye; she wanted him to take her home. She couldn't spend another minute with Ludbank without saying something that might make him into an enemy.

She sensed that Ludbank wanted to speak again as he took a deep breath beside her, but she turned to Mrs. Millspoon, who looked rather glum. "Mrs. Millspoon, how did you like the orchestra tonight?"

"Tolerable, m'dear. And the food here is always good." She threw a glance at her charge. "I believe it's time to take our leave, though it'll be difficult to tear Davina away; she's quite absorbed in conversation."

Lenore was going to say that it looked as if Charlie, too, was entranced, but she noted the glazed look in his eyes. He had finally tired of the endless chatter about frills and furbelows. She placed her hand to her forehead.

"Charlie, I'm suffering from a headache."

He glanced at her without really noticing her. "*Charlie,* will you please take me home?"

"I thought that would be my duty," Ludbank said with a sniff.

"You must take Miss Bright and Mrs. Millspoon back. They are depending on you to get home."

"That wouldn't stop me from assisting you as well, Lenore."

She sighed and pressed her fingertips to her temples. "Please, no argument. The evening has been filled with nothing but upheaval."

"That's because of that man! He's a thorn in my side."

"Nonsense! It's what you make of it." Lenore couldn't stand another minute of Ludbank's accusations. She wanted to rest her aching head on a soft pillow and time to sort out her feelings and her thoughts.

Charlie obliged her and within minutes the party had been divided and bundled into two carriages. The last Lenore saw of Ludbank was his wounded expression, and she thought Charlie should have shown more restraint when he bowed to the fair Davina. It was a relief to stare straight ahead into nothing in the dark coach.

Chapter 15

"She actually *talked* to me, Lenore," Charlie said as he joined her in the carriage. "My goddess noticed me at last." He patted her hand. "Your advice was amazingly accurate."

"How did you like the conversation? Enjoy the discourse about silks, ribbons, and tassels? Beaded reticules? Perhaps you should go into business."

"Refrain from sarcasm, Lenore. I don't know what's wrong with you." Charlie sounded peevish. "And frankly, I don't mind discussing the fal-lals of fashion."

"I see. How would that be in the long run? Imagine poring over Parisian fashion during breakfast."

"She's so lovely," he said, his voice an ocean of longing.

"Even the most tender rose must fade," she said dampeningly.

"How can you be so cruel?" he wailed, and she gritted her teeth.

"Did you arrange a rendezvous with her?"

Charlie shuddered. "I couldn't get her away from that dragon even for a minute."

"Go to her mornings at home. You can ogle her for half an hour with twenty other nincompoops."

"How can you say such things, Lenore? You are altogether heartless."

"Am I? Perhaps you deserve each other." Lenore crossed her arms over her chest. "I got this started, and now it's up to you to show her what kind of man you are."

Charlie wreaked havoc with his hair, and he moaned into his pudgy hands.

"Charlie, sit up straight! How can you only think about yourself when my brother might lose his life to that—er, murderer?"

"Eric is sure to fire in the air. I wouldn't miss any sleep over it."

The thought of the duel made her cold all over. She realized she worried about Eric as well. Her brother, when acting on temper, was prone to rashness. Dear God, why had she ever become involved, and what prompted her to continue this madness? Well, she wouldn't go any further.

End of business. Finis. Another dawn would rise tomorrow.

"The diary, ma'am," Beaton said with a hint of defeat in his voice the next morning. He held out the black-leather bound volume to her.

"Well? Did you discover—?"

"It distresses me greatly to confess that I still have not discovered the man's identity. This time, someone at the tearoom delivered the journal here. Everyone must know it belongs to you by now. It was sitting on your doorstep wrapped in a newssheet."

She took the journal and studied it front to back.

"Please bring the wrapping if you still have it. There may be a clue."

Beaton went away to obey her orders. *The whole world knows where I live,* she thought, and a chill traveled up her spine. Fatigue weighed her limbs and she thought she would never be her old self again. Ever since she'd met Eric Ramsdell she hadn't been able to sleep well. Thoughts churned through her mind endlessly, questions about Eric and his life, and Cedric, and about love.

She touched the cover of her journal, reluctant to open it and read what the stranger had written. His tone had been gentler lately, but she was never sure what to expect—an unguarded admission or another cut from the sharp side of his tongue.

Beaton returned with the covering, but as they scrutinized the pages together, they found no clues to the origin. With a look of disappointment, Beaton left the room, and Lenore slowly opened the journal.

Her breath caught in her throat as she read the entry, surprised at his sincerity and his perceptiveness. She felt a flash of tenderness for his awkwardness, and sent him a silent blessing for success with his beloved.

She went to her escritoire and sat down, spreading the fabric of her pale pink muslin gown around her. Opening the journal to the end, she gripped her quill and forced herself to concentrate.

> *I'm pleasantly surprised to hear that you're examining your emotions—or lack thereof—closely. That's the beginning of a new life, one of sensitivity and understanding.*
>
> *As you take the first awkward steps forward you may*

encounter a lot of resistance, but as you advance it will become easier and easier.

Here, Lenore wondered if she sounded condescending, but it was too late now. Crossing it out would only make a muddle of things.

I assure you that the lady of your heart will show her gratitude as you show your more tender side to her. To feel appreciated, cosseted, and loved is every lady's dream; each hopes to be the center of her beloved's life. Respect and appreciation, honesty and kindness. What more can I say? If you manage to change in those aspects as you intend, ladies will be tripping over their silk slippers to gain your favors.

You'll be surprised how much appreciation will come your way and how fast you'll find the perfect wife.

I have a little confession of my own to make. My thoughts are in turmoil, my emotions rising to the highest peaks only to plummet down to the lowest valleys, my heart beating to a faster beat, and I fight it every day. I believe I might have lost my own heart, and it bothers me no end.

She felt embarrassed to mention it, but if he could reveal his own weaknesses, why should she hold back hers? Touching her red cheeks, she glanced out the window, at the rain clouds in the sky. Thank God she didn't have to face this man who had mocked her so at the outset, and now had confessed to knowing so little about life and love. What a change, she thought, and took some pride in being the instrument for his desire to change.

I never have a problem making my opinion known, but at the same time, when my own weakness is at stake, I hide behind bravado. I prefer not to reveal my more tender emotions in front of someone else, as I am shy. I can almost hear you laugh. Shy? You scoff. Only at five o'clock in the morning, you'll say. In fact, I rarely show my more romantic side that does believe in love and honor, in poetry, and a life of happiness. If I were the woman who had ignited your heart, would you take the time to stop and really see me? Would you always think you know what is best for me, or believe that what you do for me is enough?

Would you even think to ask?

The words surprised Lenore as well. She knew to what length she would go to accommodate a husband or lover, as she had for Ronald, but she doubted a gentleman would ever do that for her. It was something she had accepted, yet she longed for a kindred soul.

Why inflict hurt, or exchange angry words, when love was all that mattered? She could hear him laugh again. He would say her belief was unrealistic, and that no living soul could ever be so perfect. In her mind it was simple. All it would take was willingness and patience.

She picked up her quill and sharpened it, and then proceeded to repeat that last thought of *willingness and patience* at the end of her entry. After that she didn't really have anything else to say.

Curiously enough, the correspondence seemed to be over; it had come full circle. It surely felt that way, and perhaps it was good that she didn't know who her correspondent had been. Faced with the person, she might not have dared to reveal herself as she had.

Still, the mystery intrigued her no end.

With a sigh, she sanded the pages. What now? If she left the diary on her own doorstep, and set a footman to watch over it, the stranger would not appear.

She suspected he would look for the book at the Rose Tearoom, and that's where she would leave it. This time she wouldn't even bother to ask Beaton to keep an eye on the comings and goings there. She had no need to know who her correspondent was, not really.

Belinda visited her in the afternoon, and Lenore shared the latest events with her. "They are meeting at dawn tomorrow. I've never been more mortified."

"Perhaps you shouldn't have walked down that dark path with Mr. Ramsdell. The fact that you did was a blatant invitation to these kinds of difficulties."

"Edward will hardly speak to me after this. You know how he fumes."

Belinda nodded, yet her expression spoke of slight disapproval. "Can you really blame him? Your way-wardness must infuriate him no end. He's a stickler for propriety, after all."

"I'm more aware of it than most," Lenore said. She scrutinized her friend closely, noting the paleness of her cheeks. "Belinda, what's the matter?"

"Do you recall what I told you in confidence in the park?"

"Of course. I sense your troubled heart."

"Adam discovered my secret, and then my lover ran away. I fear that Adam threatened him, or he was a coward and fled before Adam reached him. I warned him, you see."

"Poor dear," Lenore said and pulled her friend

close. She gently patted Belinda's back as she started crying.

"It was the most difficult thing to discover that he has truly left."

"Ought he to have stayed and fought with Adam?"

"Yes . . . well, perhaps. I wouldn't want to see him dead. Adam was so very vexed, but he well understands that our marriage is a sham. I reasoned I could have lovers just as he has his opera dancers."

"That's altogether different."

Belinda pressed her face against Lenore's shoulder. "It is monstrously unfair."

Lenore nodded, unable to embroider more on that statement. "You'll get over this man. He wasn't courageous enough to stand up for your love."

"I doubt that anyone would be."

"Well, in the eyes of Society, a woman's adultery is a serious matter," Lenore said matter-of-factly. She gripped her friend's shoulders and gently pushed her away. Giving her a clean handkerchief from her pocket, Lenore continued. "Let's take a drive into the country tomorrow. I want to go to the village where Cedric died."

"Why dredge up all that sorrow?" Belinda asked and dabbed at her eyes.

"I want to know the truth of what really happened."

"You long to clear Mr. Ramsdell's name," Belinda said.

Lenore didn't hesitate. "Perhaps."

"I'll go with you unless Adam locks me up. He's sending me to Chandler Hall at the end of the week." Belinda's tears dried, but her blue eyes were rimmed in red. "So you're not going to watch the duelers?"

Lenore gave an unladylike snort. "Of course not!

They can wave pistols at each other as they've got nothing better to do."

Belinda nodded and righted the small cap on top of her head. She looked like a bedraggled kitten. "Good riddance to all of them."

"The outing will do you good, Belinda."

"I daresay."

Chapter 16

Eric shivered in the cool and damp morning air. The sun was rising over the trees, chasing away the fog over the field at Barn Elms. The grass grew tall and vigorous, interspersed with buttercups and bachelor buttons. Dew hung on every branch and every leaf.

"Dashed nuisance to be abroad at this ungodly hour," Charlie said, his chin buried in a scarf. "Where are the others?"

"I hear horses. I hope all the ruckus won't alert the authorities," Eric said with a grim feeling.

Charlie shaded his eyes from the golden morning sunlight. "They are all riding together."

"That doesn't surprise me. It looks as if they brought two seconds each." Eric, too, shaded his eyes. "Look, there's a coach coming behind. I'll wager it's the surgeon they bribed to be here. I daresay they're aiming to draw some blood this morning."

Charlie didn't look too pleased. "Blood makes me squeamish." He glanced at Eric's white shirtfront under his open greatcoat. "You are an easy target."

"So are they." Eric didn't worry in the least. He actually didn't care if he lived or died at this point. He had hoped to pursue his romance with Lenore and see where it would lead, but if it hadn't happened, well, he had no unfinished business. His grandparents would mourn him, and there would always be a dark spot on the family name, but unless he could clear the past, there would be whether he lived or died.

Charlie lifted Eric's arm by the wrist and studied his hand on both sides. "By Gad, it's steady! I would tremble so much my teeth would chatter."

Eric laughed at that. "It's unlikely you would find yourself in a situation like this, Charlie. You are the most amiable person I know."

Charlie shrugged, his forehead creased with worry. "Eric, I pray this is the last duel you're part of."

"Oh—do you want me to die this morning?" Eric chided.

Charlie's jaw fell open. "Damn it, no! What I mean is that I'd like to hear some good news from you, and not be forced to witness more of these dismal encounters because you have provoked someone and you have no other friends."

Eric was going to protest, but he knew the man was right. "It's time for some good news, Charlie. Let's handle these two firebrands and spend the rest of the day finding something good."

Charlie shook his head and made a face. "You confound me, but at least I'm never bored in your presence."

The other men joined them, horses snorting and slogging through the grass. Next, Denbury and Ludbank tied them to one of the low-hanging branches of the gigantic elm growing at the edge of the clearing. There was a self-righteous light in their eyes as they approached Eric and Charlie. The seconds came next, equally grim expressions on their faces.

"Good morning, gentlemen." Eric greeted them with

a smile, which was not well received. "Do remember you're not heading for the guillotine."

"We might as well be," Denbury snapped. "Or you are."

Eric braced his hands on his hips. "We're meeting at dawn when we could still be sleeping in our own beds. 'Tis a stupid custom."

Denbury growled, and Eric realized his mistake too late. "Custom? We meet to get a painful wound somewhere on our bodies—at dawn? I'd say it's damned inconvenient."

Ludbank looked as if he had blood on his mind too—Eric's. "Show us the weapons," he snarled.

Charlie hurried to gather the case of Mantons from a cloth he'd spread on the ground. They inspected the fine pistols carefully, and the seconds weighed the lead balls as if some injustice could be found there. Eric knew they were perfectly balanced, the triggers at the ready. A man with a deadly aim holding a Manton could do much damage.

"I dislike this charade," Eric began. They only glared at him, tempers rising.

"I realize you caught me kissing Mrs. Andrews, but she's of age—"

"But she's not *yours!*" Ludbank shouted.

"Not yours either," Eric drawled as he watched the seconds load the pistols. "You've sadly misjudged the situation."

"She will be after you're gone," Ludbank yelled, startling a cloud of blackbirds out of their sleep in the bushes.

"Shh, you'll have the authorities breathing down our necks. Do you want to spend the rest of your life in exile? If you kill me, that's what you'll have to do, and I'm certain Mrs. Andrews won't follow you to the Continent."

Ludbank grumbled something. It was clear he hadn't thought that far ahead. Denbury gave Eric a glare that promised nothing but misery and a terrible end. Eric laughed inwardly. The fools didn't know he'd already died a few deaths.

"For me it's about Cedric," Denbury said, with a glimmer of honesty. "I can't control what my sister does, however much I might wish to do so. Her willful behavior often infuriates me."

"Perhaps she dares to express herself in a world where females have no room to do so."

"There are degrees of expression," Denbury said icily. "And she has a duty to the Brigham name."

"I'd say she comports herself with great dignity, and she's certainly an asset to your family."

Ludbank muttered something to that effect, and Eric noted his divided loyalty. "Well, if you can't solve this peacefully, let's get it done. I'm damned tired of standing here in the cold waiting to get shot."

The seconds gave him looks of disapproval, but he didn't care. They finished loading and gave one of the pistols to Ludbank, the other to Eric.

They went to stand in the middle of the meadow, backs touching. Eric felt his adversary's tension, and he focused on the treetops ahead. The wooden stock of the Manton lay smooth and hard in his hand, the barrel pointing toward the sky.

"On the count of twelve," one of the seconds said. "One . . . two . . . three . . ."

Eric stepped mechanically forward, his top boots swishing against the grass.

"Twelve!"

They stopped and turned around. Ludbank's white shirtfront gleamed in the morning light, sharp against the velvet green of the grass.

"When I drop my handkerchief."

Eric took aim a good foot outside of Ludbank's right shoulder. As the handkerchief fluttered to the ground, two deafening shots rang out. He could feel the whistle and the stir in his hair as Ludbank's ball just missed his head. At that moment he knew death had been very close, but Ludbank was an inferior shot.

A moment of stillness fell, and Eric felt the icy breeze of the other man's dislike across the meadow. He had made an enemy, and that fact wasn't likely to change anytime soon. It didn't matter in the greater scheme of things.

Ludbank swore, somehow fouling the crystal-clear morning light. Eric marched back to the seconds, who had primed another set of Mantons. This pair was Denbury's. "Charlie, did you inspect the pistols?"

Charlie nodded. "They are excellent."

Denbury had tossed his coat to the ground and rolled up his sleeves. *He means business,* Eric thought. *He does have much more reason than Ludbank.* In fact, it surprised Eric that Ludbank had tried to kill him.

"Denbury, give me another chance to prove my innocence. Cedric didn't die at my hand." He held the other man's gaze earnestly, and Denbury had a moment of hesitation, then shrugged it off. Eric saw his determination in the thinning of his mouth.

"Let's get on with it then, I'm cold," Eric said, and the procedure repeated itself. He counted his breaths even as they stepped the twelve steps. He had a feeling that Denbury was a much better shot than Ludbank.

The cool clarity of Denbury's gaze hit him across the expanse of the mist-wreathed meadow.

The handkerchief dropped, and Eric shot far wide of his mark.

He braced himself for the impact, but nothing happened. Eric stared at the raised pistol aimed at his heart. Denbury intended to make him sweat, and a cold sweat did indeed break out all over his body, but still he stared fearlessly at his opponent.

"What are you waiting for?" he shouted, as the pistol remained mute.

The aim wavered, and then Denbury's arm went down. Ludbank swore again as he watched.

"What's wrong, Edward? Blast the man's head off!"

"I'll do so later."

Denbury walked off the field and Eric followed. At the site where the seconds waited, Denbury turned to Eric. "I give you one chance to prove your innocence, all in the name of your friendship with Cedric, but if we prove you guilty once and for all, I shall hunt you down with no mercy."

Eric gave a curt nod. "Thank you."

Denbury turned his back.

Eric respected the man for giving him that small glimmer of hope. This might be the beginning of a more peaceful end to the tragedy of Cedric's death. "I will give my utmost effort to prove my innocence." It was on the tip of his tongue to say who *had* killed Cedric, but since he couldn't prove it, there was no point.

He could however drop a hint. "Cedric made enemies at the gaming tables—one of them was Sir Winton Niles. He lost a fortune to Cedric, as I'm sure you're aware. He carried a grudge."

Denbury still had his back turned, and Eric could see the tension stiffening every muscle. "Ramsdell, don't cast blame elsewhere to confuse the issue." His voice dripped with ice. "I was well aware of Cedric's gambling. It was deplorable, to say the least, and ruinous to others."

"My point precisely," Eric said.

Denbury pulled on his jacket and gave Eric a hard, searching stare.

"It's evident you never looked at that angle, Denbury."

"No need to."

Eric had a protest on the tip of his tongue, but kept it in check. He joined Charlie, who looked hugely relieved. "Let's go, old fellow. We've done our work here."

Climbing into Charlie's coach, they left the meadow.

"Phew, a close call, Eric." Charlie wiped his forehead with a handkerchief. "Ludbank meant business."

"Denbury does understand fair play."

"He's a decent fellow, if a bit rash. He and Ludbank both have fierce tempers and I would not want to be at the receiving end of their wrath."

"Well, you probably will be just by associating with me," Eric said with a sigh.

"Don't be a fool. I know you would never kill anyone, and the world will know soon too. Isn't there something we can do?"

"Yes, let's fetch our horses and ride down to Rope-hill village on the Brighton road. I know that Sir Winton Niles kept a mistress there sometime ago, a Miss Sharp. It has occurred to me that that's how he disappeared from the area so quickly after the shooting. He just laid low until the tragedy was over and the militia stopped searching for possible suspects."

"You've never mentioned this before."

"What's the use, Charlie? I've confronted Winton a number of times, but he laughs in my face, the bounder. I've been down this road before. His mistress wouldn't divulge any information to me, but she might now. I believe Winton is dying. He's bedridden and increasingly jaundiced. Too many late nights with the opium and the brandy bottles."

"Hmm, we've seen numerous fellows go down that slippery path."

Eric nodded, thoughtful. The coach sped through the city toward Mayfair, passing milk wagons and farmers' carts along the way. "Charlie, Denbury was an inch from killing me. I'm surprised he hasn't called me out before."

"He didn't have the opportunity."

"He could've sought me out at Swinmere, or here in London."

"Well, as you just found out, he seems to think that you just might be telling the truth. You can't go around shooting men simply because you're angry. Denbury will listen to reason; he's not an idiot."

Eric leaned his head back against the squabs and closed his eyes. "I'm tired, Charlie. This matter has to end soon."

Charlie leaned over and patted Eric's arm. "It will, my friend, it will."

Lenore and Belinda arrived at the posting inn, the Red Pheasant, on the outskirts of Ropehill. The day had turned hot and the air hung dense and still, promising a storm. Lenore was battling a headache, and her gown clung to her damp skin. Her thoughts moved in an unbreakable orbit of worry about Eric.

Had Edward shot him in a duel this morning, or had Ludbank? Worse still, had more than one man been shot? She couldn't bear the thought of something happening to her brother.

"Let's find some refreshments," she said to Belinda, who agreed with vigor.

Lenore shook off the doldrums and banged on the hatch with the crook of her umbrella, and Beaton's kindly face—or part of it—appeared in the small opening. Lenore had asked him to join them in the interests of propriety. Edward would be proud of her prudence, she thought.

"Beaton, a pitcher of lemonade, please."

"Yes, ma'am." He hastened to get down from the box and opened the door, folding down the step so that the ladies could get down. Dust whirled across the hard-packed dirt in the stable yard. Horses stomped along the wall, patrons sitting in the shade of large oaks surrounding the inn. The half-timbered building had latticed windows, which stood open to let in what air there was. A serving wench moved between tables, cleaning the wooden surfaces with a damp rag.

"Should I call for a private parlor?" Beaton asked before heading into the taproom.

"No"—Lenore looked at Belinda—"I'd rather stay outside, don't you?"

"Yes," Belinda replied. "I brought a sketchbook and these elegant trees would make a good subject to sketch."

Lenore looked around the ordinary yard, which looked much the same as always. "This is the last place Cedric stopped before the . . . accident," she said, tears gathering hot in her throat.

"I know. I don't quite understand why you want to dig up that old pain, Lenore."

"I should like to discover what really happened that day."

"Only because you have a *tendre* for Eric Ramsdell."

Lenore felt a spurt of annoyance. "You're right. I shan't deny it. However, only one person should have to protest the false accusations for the Law to investigate more thoroughly."

"We know they questioned everyone here, and in the surrounding area. What they saw was Eric leaving straight after Cedric had pulled back onto the road. He was in hot pursuit. Granted, they were in the middle of a race, but it's said that Eric was so set on winning that—"

"That's ridiculous," Lenore said with a dismissive wave of her hand.

"Perhaps it is, but I'm trying to reason it out."

"It is difficult . . . if not impossible." Lenore sat down on a wooden bench in the shade under a tree and folded up her umbrella. Leaning it against the tree trunk, she began to fan her hot face. Chickens scratched in the dirt and chased each other as they competed for choice morsels. A striped cat sunned itself on the stone steps leading to the taproom. Beaton came out and hastened across the yard to them.

"Lemonade will be forthcoming. I took the liberty of ordering some freshly baked almond cakes as well."

Lenore smiled. "Thank you, Beaton."

He took a seat on a bench nearby, and as the serving wench brought the lemonade, she brought a mug of ale for him.

"Ladies," she said with a curtsy and placed her tray on the adjacent table. She wore a mobcap over her brown curls and brown serge gown, with a pristine apron over her sturdy middle. She poured the cool liquid into glasses and handed them out.

"Have you worked here long?" Lenore asked.

"Two years, milady." She gave Lenore a curious glance as though she found it strange that a person of quality would address her in any way except to give orders.

"Quite a lovely spot," Lenore said. "Were you here when that young man was murdered not far from here?"

"Oh, yes." The young woman paled. "It was 'orrible, milady. When 'e stopped 'ere, 'e gave me a whole shillin' extra for serving 'im a tankard of ale, and 'e pinched me chin, sayin' I was pretty."

"That sounds like Cedric," Belinda said dryly.

"Inebriated no doubt," Lenore said.

"Aye, milady, 'e was deeply in 'is cups, almost to a point of fallin' orf that peculiar 'igh carriage o' 'is."

"A high-perch phaeton," Lenore explained.

"I was that sad t' 'ear 'e'd been killed."

"Did you see that other gentleman who they say shot him?" Lenore continued, fearing the reply.

"Aye, 'e stopped 'ere too, a well-mannered gent who spoke kindly to me." She leaned closer. "They argued, y'know, right 'ere in the yard before takin' off."

Lenore's heart beat faster. "Do you know what the argument was about?"

"The second gent didn't like that nice Mr. Brigham to drink anymore. 'E said th' drink would kill 'im— and, Lud, it did."

"If that was the case, that he cared, why would he then go and shoot the man?" Lenore wanted to hear the woman's opinion.

"'Twas a ruse, that's all. 'E wanted to look kind and concerned, but 'e kept viperish thoughts close to 'is chest, and as soon as 'e saw 'is chance, 'e pulled out 'is pistol and fired."

Lenore sighed. She could see no hope for Eric Ramsdell. Their love story had been doomed from the start.

Chapter 17

Lenore looked at the serving maid and noticed her earnest expression. The woman wouldn't have any reason to lie. Her spirits plummeted even further, but she took a swallow of the lemonade and asked, "Did you see anyone else involved in the race?" Fishing in her reticule, she found sixpence and gave it to the maid, who accepted it gratefully.

"Not in the race, milady. Sumthin' was strange, though. An urchin, I don't know 'is name or where 'e came from, but 'e appeared 'ere and 'anded the gent wot died a note, and then disappeared. The constables were lookin' for 'im, but no one saw 'im again."

"Hmm, he must've been from other parts," Lenore said. "But he obviously knew that Mr. Brigham was coming through this way and waited."

"Aye . . . a boy about ten and all alone."

"Someone must've waited for him and taken him away from here," Belinda said.

Lenore nodded. "I would have liked to have read that note."

"Yes, but there was no mention of one in the investigation," Belinda said.

"The killer took it away," the maid said with a sad tinge in her voice.

"However, why would the second gentleman write Mr. Brigham a note and then go and shoot him?" Lenore pointed out.

The maid pursed her lips in thought. "That's a question an' all."

"More than likely it was the latest information about the size of the bets that had been laid. Quite a sum of money was at stake here," Lenore said. "Perhaps someone was pushing Cedric to win."

"Well, 'e *won* all right," the maid said morosely. She curtsied again and went back to the taproom.

Lenore drank more of the tart lemonade. Horses were pulling into the yard, kicking up a great cloud of dust that mixed with the dirty brown of the darkening sky. A storm was looming. Two riders clattered up to the stables, and a groom came to take the reins. Dark stains of perspiration covered the mounts' hides as if they'd been ridden hard. The riders dismounted and began walking toward the inn and Lenore's heart almost stopped when she recognized Eric and Charlie. What were *they* doing here?

At least Eric had not been killed. She rose from the bench, and the men saw her simultaneously. Charlie gave out a whoop. "Fancy that! It's a small world."

Lenore waved, relief making her legs tremble.

Eric smiled, clearly happy to see her, and she smiled back, like a fool. He bowed before her and kissed her hand.

"I'm glad to see you well," she said with heartfelt concern in her voice.

"Never better," he replied and greeted Belinda.

"And my brother?" Lenore continued.

"Everyone celebrated a peaceful morning—over huge breakfasts, no doubt," Eric replied.

"We had a very early start," Charlie said, "but we never expected to run into you at Ropehill."

"'Tis rather odd," Eric said.

"We took a ride in the carriage, but the weather is threatening in the west. We had to stop here for some lemonade before returning to London." Lenore thought the excuse sounded thin. "In fact, I wanted to visit where Cedric was last seen alive, although I've been here before."

"You're only torturing yourself, Lenore," Charlie said. "It won't bring Cedric back."

"I realize that. Nevertheless—"

"You have been here before too, Mr. Ramsdell," Belinda stated coolly.

"Ah, yes . . . that I have. It was a most disturbing day, the worst of my life, in fact." He stood with his hands behind his back as if waiting for more judgments, but everyone remained awkwardly silent.

"Have a glass of lemonade," Lenore said and gestured at the pitcher.

"Not for me," Eric said. "I'd rather have some ale."

The serving wench came outside and approached the party. She gasped when she saw Eric. "You!" She turned her shocked gaze at Lenore. "We were just talkin' about 'im."

Eric lifted his eyebrows in surprise.

"Yes," Lenore said. "I'm as shocked to see him as you are."

"Fetch us some ale," Charlie demanded to smooth over the awkwardness.

The maid fled back to the taproom.

"She'll think we're hatching some conspiracy or plot," Lenore said.

"You asked her questions about me?" Eric asked, his voice reserved.

"Yes, we asked if you'd been seen here the day Cedric died," Lenore said, and was glad she dared to be honest. Truth be told, she only sought to help him, but he couldn't know that.

"It's evident I was hot on his heels in the race."

Lenore couldn't quite read his expression, and the intimacy they'd shared was gone. Had it all been a dream? He looked so handsome in his blue riding coat and buckskins, his face immobile, and his brown eyes shadowed with pain. He met her gaze squarely, as if waiting for her next statement or question. She longed to touch his hair and smooth the worry from his forehead.

"Why are you two here?" she asked.

"I have perhaps a small chance to clear my name. There's someone in this area I want to see," he explained. "All avenues have been explored, but there's always a possibility someone missed some details."

"And I'm here to lend moral support," Charlie said, "something I do quite often, it seems." He sat down on the bench next to Lenore and nodded toward Beaton. "At least you're not haring around the county without a male protector."

"Beaton claims to be rather a fierce pugilist and Bob, the coachman, is a veritable giant, and then there's the footman—do you want me to go on?"

Charlie shook his head. "I'm extremely pleased to hear that you have some sense, Lenore."

Raindrops spattered the yard; before long the sky would open up. They were safe for a few minutes under the oak, but it would be safer to take refuge in the building.

Lenore gathered her parasol. "Come, Belinda, let's go inside."

They ran across the yard to the taproom. The air was filled with tobacco smoke and the odors of cooking food. Eric stopped right behind her, and she felt his strength as support. Charlie found a table in the back, separated from the main area with a screen. He led Belinda there and dusted off the bench. Lenore started to follow, but Eric halted her. Some locals drinking ale followed their progress with curiosity.

He pulled her aside, and they stood near a window, staring at the sheets of rain sweeping the yard. "I would like you to know that you coming into my life has given me new life," he whispered. "Before I made your acquaintance, I didn't care what happened to me. I had resigned myself to the life of an outcast, but now I want to reclaim my good name. You have been my inspiration."

She blushed. "I'm happy that I have made a difference. I realize times are difficult for you, but the truth will out if you're innocent."

He touched a tendril of her hair that had blown loose. Tenderness softened his features, and drowned in his eyes. "Lenore, I would like to kiss you with great passion right now and hold you so tight you could barely breathe."

She couldn't control a giggle, her hand covering her mouth. Self-conscious and wondering if she'd heard aright, and heart hammering in her chest, she met his caressing gaze. "You're taking my breath away," she whispered. He couldn't know that his words were melting her reserve. Guilt and pleasure mingled within her, and she wished he were just a regular fellow, not someone with the label of murderer—Cedric's killer—attached to his name.

"A few bribes might bring me the information I need," he said. "Time has passed and the person whom I believe protected the killer in the past might have changed her mind."

"Do you know something the authorities don't?"

"Yes, I'm certain of the identity of the man who shot Cedric, but I haven't been able to prove it." He must have noticed her curiosity. "You don't know him, Lenore."

She settled for that, but she would ask him more questions later, in a more private setting.

His gaze caressed her some more, warming her blood anew. "You're teaching me about love," he murmured. "Every time we are together becomes a lesson in patience and curiosity. Patience because I can't just sweep you in my arms and carry you away, and curiosity about what makes the attraction so strong. Why am I drawn to you, and not a thousand others? And how do I get to know you—the mystery that is you?"

She laughed. "I am only a woman. Flighty. Frivolous—"

"That you are not," he said. "You have many layers and deep thoughts that inspire me more than you can imagine."

"How do you know?" His statement surprised her.

He looked disconcerted for a moment as, if catching himself in a lie, but her mind must be playing tricks on her. "I . . . er, I feel I know you, yet I don't," he said lamely.

Odd. That was how she felt about the stranger

who wrote in her journal; she knew him intimately, but not at all. "I suppose it's possible if one is good at guessing."

He stared into the distance, his face pensive and—uncomfortable. Why would he look uncomfortable? Perhaps intimacy embarrassed him, she thought.

"I . . . well, there are things I've done that I'm not proud of," he said haltingly. "Sometimes rash decisions make for great advantage, sometimes they will come back to haunt you."

"I don't know what you're talking about."

He sighed. "I suppose I was speaking more to myself than to you. Still, my decision to approach you when you didn't want to have anything to do with me proved to be sound."

She smiled. "I daresay it was, but it doesn't help us now, does it? Edward will never forgive you, and by speaking with you like this—against his wishes, I seem to mock his grief. I find that I have to avoid you to respect his wishes."

"If I'm cleared, I shall approach your brother myself. He would expect that of me. If I can't prove my innocence, he'll finish what he didn't this morning. I was a trigger pull from death."

"Edward is a good man, but a stubborn one." She looked over her shoulder to where Belinda sat with Charlie. "I'd better join my friends. We have been doing a bit of questioning ourselves, but nothing has come to light."

He nodded. "It probably won't, but thank you for wanting to help me and making the effort to find the truth."

"It's the principle of the thing." She patted his arm and went across the room.

* * *

He watched her straight, slender back and wished he could hold her in his arms and never let go. The agony of his deceit concerning the diary marred every encounter with her now. How could he confess the truth without losing her? She would never forgive him, she who set such store by honesty and trust. He did, too, now that he'd met her. Before, it wasn't something that overly concerned him. Everything would have to be aboveboard with her.

He wondered if she'd returned the diary to the tearoom this morning. He hadn't had the time to retrieve it.

Charlie joined him. "The rain is letting up. Shall we proceed?"

Eric nodded. "Yes, we might as well." He threw a longing look at Lenore, and she returned his scrutiny. With a small wave of her hand, she smiled as if to wish him good luck.

Buoyed by her support, he went out into the steaming yard. A rainbow had formed in the aftermath of the storm, and he took that as a good omen. "Onward, Charlie. The infamous Minette Sharp lives at the far end of the village."

They rode along the lane, the horses stepping through the rain puddles. Birds fluttered or swooped, landing on branches nearby, scattering raindrops in every direction. The sunlight created a kaleidoscope of colors in the water. A farmer and his wife were out in a field working, and they waved as the men rode by.

Smoke was coming out of Minette's chimney, and Eric pulled up to the whitewashed house. Unkempt roses grew along the dilapidated walls. One of her ad-

mirers must have put her up here, or bought her the
cottage as payment for her intimate services. As an
opera dancer, she had led a dissolute life, but now a
matronly woman in a high-necked gown opened the
door for them. Eric barely recognized her changed
appearance. She still had a beautiful face, with high
cheekbones, a pretty mouth, and long, curly eyelashes.

"Minette? I was expecting red hair and a low-cut
dress?" He bowed to her.

She frowned, her mouth thinning into a hard line.
"Mr. Ramsdell. That woman is dead and buried. I am
a respectable woman in this community."

"I daresay the upstanding citizens of Ropehill
wouldn't accept anything less." He turned to Charlie.
"This is my friend Charlie Minion."

"If you two are looking for favors, there are none to
be had here," she snapped and began to close the
door.

Eric braced his arm against it. "We're not here for
that, and we won't keep you but a minute."

She opened the door anew. "What is it then? Are
you bringing news from London?"

"Yes . . . I visited Sir Winton Niles the other day. I
believe he's dying; he has a wasting illness by the looks
of it."

"I wouldn't know. I haven't seen him for a long time,
and I'm surprised he would accept a visit from you."

"He didn't exactly accept it, but I made him. You
know of the crime that happened outside Ropehill,
and I believe you were protecting Winton at the time
of Cedric Brigham's death." He pointed at the cottage. "I don't blame you for that if he is footing the
bill for this."

She laughed, a raucous sound that didn't sound

ladylike at all. "Win never gave me as much as a corsage for my bodice. The skinflint used me and threw me away. I loved him, which was the silliest thing I've ever done."

"I see."

"You don't see anything, Mr. Ramsdell."

"What do you mean?"

"You're just another one of the London rakehells who cares for no one but himself." She tossed her head back in defiance.

"I used to be, but like you, I've changed." He leaned his shoulder against the doorframe. "The authorities must have been here and asked you questions, as they addressed everyone in the village."

She nodded. "Yes, but it's of no importance."

"Didn't they ask you about the identity of your gentleman friend?"

"No, they didn't. Besides, Win had left. He didn't stay here but a day."

"Just to hide long enough to avoid the authorities when they scoured the village for suspects. I had to take the full blame because they found no one."

"You knew he was here?"

"I suspected as much. And Cedric received a note, which mysteriously disappeared after his death."

"He might have dropped it somewhere. The wind has a tendency to blow things astray."

"Be that as it may, did Winton write that note?"

She thought for a moment, clearly reluctant to speak, yet not caring about protecting her erstwhile lover.

"Please, Minette, I need your help. I want to clear my name before Winton dies and all the evidence with him. Would you stand up for me—for the truth?"

"And possibly implicate myself?" She laughed. "Not bloody likely. Besides, I don't owe you anything."

"I know you don't, but in the name of new beginnings and in the name of fairness. Please, Minette."

She pursed her lips and gave him a hard stare. "Very well, Win wrote that note right here at the kitchen table. He met Cedric at the spot where Cedric died, and then you came along. Simple. Win knew you would get blamed for the crime and that suited him just fine."

"He's a cruel man."

"I had immense love for him once, but he destroyed that and then he used all of my secrets to control me. He ruined my life, but I managed to get out from under his tyranny." A shadow of worry crossed over her face. "If he finds out that I told you this, he'll kill me, or have me killed."

"He's so ill he can't rise from his bed."

"But he can hire someone."

"And pay that person?" Eric shook his head. "Winton is destitute."

"He'll raise the devil if need be." She walked backward across the threshold. Charlie barred her from closing the door in their faces.

"Ma'am," he said, "I witnessed what you had to say, but would you be willing to speak with the authorities so that Eric can clear his name?"

"And put myself forth as someone who hobnobbed with a murderer? No. I won't do that. I'm surprised I even told you the truth. You caught me at a weak moment."

"It's an immense relief for me," Eric said, "but I could use your help with the authorities. I'll make it worthwhile. How much would it be worth to you?"

She got a calculating look in her steely gray eyes. "If

you can't wring the truth out of Winton before he dies, I'll help you for five hundred pounds."

"What?" Charlie cried. "Are you gone mad?"

"Take it or leave it. I have to think about the future, and protectors aren't easy to come by when you live a respectable life."

"You need to find a husband," Eric said. "I agree to the terms. I need a witness when I visit Winton again."

"You'll have to find a way to frighten him into confessing the truth," Minette said. "He's deathly afraid of ending up in hell."

"That's where his destiny lies," Eric said flatly. "He should've thought of that before he resorted to murder."

"Play upon his fears. Tell him his soul might be redeemed if he confesses the truth."

"Yes . . . thank you. By the way, did he hide the murder weapon here?"

She shook her head. "No, I never saw any kind of weapon. He must have got rid of it after the crime."

Eric bowed. "I'm more grateful than I can say."

She shrugged her shoulders and closed the door. They were once again alone with the flowers and the bumblebees.

They left, closing the wooden gate behind them.

"What do you think, Eric? Is she telling the truth?"

"Yes, I'm sure of it."

"I'll choke the words out of Sir Winton myself," Charlie said, his voice tight with anger.

"The man cared for nothing except his own gain, and he hated to lose at the card tables. I'm surprised Cedric deigned to gamble with him."

"Cedric gambled with anyone. He loved the risk, as in all things he did. It was like a sickness."

"Possibly, but it's not important any longer."
"Where to next, Eric?"
"Winton's lair."

Chapter 18

They rode back to the Red Pheasant, only to discover that the ladies had left the inn shortly before they arrived.

"We can overtake their carriage and escort them back to London," Charlie suggested, "and perhaps you'll have a chance to explain things to Lenore."

"Yes, but Minette's claim still has to be proved. Winton will have to confess in front of witnesses."

"Yes . . . and if he doesn't?"

Eric was silent for a long moment. "I don't think about that."

"Take Lenore with you to his lodgings. If she hears his confession, she'll know the truth at last."

"I wouldn't want to expose her to the filth in which Winton lives. Anything that Winton touches gets soiled with his meanness."

"Your honor is at stake here. A little dirt won't frighten Lenore."

"She might not believe my claim that Winton is the murderer."

"She must know the truth. I believe she'll listen to you."

They rode quickly north and soon caught up with the coach that was carrying the ladies. They had stopped by the side of the road and sat under a huge oak, drinking lemonade. The grass still glittered from the recent rainstorm, but it was dry under the oak.

Lenore stared at Eric in silent inquiry.

"I had some success," he said, "but nothing conclusive. Perhaps the suspect will confess in your presence, that is, if you are willing to listen."

"That is hoping for too much," Lenore said. "Why would anyone who has not been formally accused stand up and proclaim his guilt?"

"He's in very poor health, and might want to confess before it's too late."

She pondered his words, and he shifted his weight on his feet, wondering if he would ever have a chance to clear his name. Winton was Eric's only hope right now, and Winton would only sell information, not give it away. As Lenore said, why would he implicate himself? Winton was a dangerous man. *I'm forced to confront him again,* Eric thought.

The sun shone hotly above, and he peered through the branches at the clear sky.

He longed to dally here in the grass with Lenore, but the tension of the moment prevented any kind of lighthearted camaraderie. She hadn't offered to join him or to be a witness. He made up his mind to return to London posthaste.

"I have business to attend to," he said curtly and motioned to Charlie to join him. "Lenore, I shall contact you in due course, and you will finally know the whole truth, as will your brother."

She nodded, and he sensed her frustration as keenly as his own. He planted a kiss on her hand, and knew she didn't mind it in the least. Belinda stared at him with hard eyes, but did not pull away when he kissed her hand as well. His feelings for Lenore must be obvious to everyone.

Back in London he parted with Charlie and rode back to Berkely Square. He discovered that the servants had recovered Lenore's diary yet again, and he sat down to read it just as soon as he'd peeled off his gloves.

She confessed to having fallen in love. He wanted to believe he was the object of her affections but he rejected such an impossibility. She was asking if he would really hear her and acknowledge her needs. The question was one he'd never heard before, but the answer was not a mystery. Her comforts were important to him, and of course he would take the time to listen to her—because he loved her, and he wanted to understand her.

If he could reply yes to all of these questions, he would gain her approval. He prayed he was her secret love.

The problem of his subterfuge still troubled him. When she discovered that he was also her secret correspondent, would she ever forgive him? Did she have to find out? Life would be much easier if she didn't, but could he live with the knowledge of his own deception?

Oh, just thinking about it made him blue-deviled. He would have to write to her for the last time and end this charade. Carrying the book with him, he went to his bedchamber, where he sat down at the desk.

Sharpening a quill, he thought about what to write.

> *You have confessed your feelings in a most tender fashion, which makes my heart beat faster. It delights me no end to hear that the woman whose heart I thought was made of stone has deep feelings after all. You worry about the gentleman not seeing you for who you are, but how could he not? Any man would consider himself exceedingly fortunate to claim your tender heart.*

*You have whetted my curiosity: Who is this paragon?
Perhaps you cannot answer, lest you give away your secret, but I have become your friend through all this.*

*However, it is with a heavy heart that I tell you we
must cease this correspondence. Once you're promised
to another, it wouldn't be right to keep up an exchange
with a secret admirer. Yes, that's who I am. The dis-
dain I showed in the beginning is no more. I shall no
longer blindly follow current customs as I once did.
You have taught me to believe in love.*

*Though it can be frightening to reveal your weak-
nesses, no one will ever quite know you if you do
not—least of all the man who is closest to your heart.*

*I have grown very fond of you but I know I cannot
hope for more. Since you are now involved with someone else, we must cease to write each other and
concentrate on the people who matter the most. I'll miss
your refreshing candor, but at the same time, I'll know
you've softened, and that you're happy. I rejoice in that
knowledge and I wish you the stars, I wish you happiness and the best of everything because you deserve it!*

He thought it was a good ending—affectionate but
to the point. Once more, he vowed to keep the secret
of the diary. There was no need for her to know, or to
grow wrathful once again at him. They had quarreled
enough as it was.

Sighing, he put aside the quill and the diary. He
would miss their confrontations and their confessions.
Tired, he lay down and soon fell into an uneasy sleep.
It was dark when he awakened, and he had barely
changed into an evening coat when Charlie stormed
into his bedchamber.

"Is there a fire somewhere?" Eric drawled and adjusted his cravat. "In your coattails perhaps?"

"Of course not," Charlie retorted. "I encountered the fair Davina on Bond Street this afternoon, and she's going to the Lyttons' for dinner tonight. I was invited there too. Perhaps this will be the night when Davina sees my sterling qualities and swoons with tender feelings."

"That is, if she has any," Eric said dampeningly.

Charlie didn't listen. He stared at himself in the mirror. "I came here to have you arrange my neck cloth. No one better for the job."

Eric smiled. "I'm glad I'm good for something."

"I shall conquer her tonight. Our engagement will be in all the papers by next week. I doubt that her father will have any objections to the match."

Eric lifted his eyebrows. "Have you approached him?"

"No, it did seem farfetched that Davina would notice me, let alone consider me for a husband, but after that evening at Vauxhall, I am much more confident."

"I daresay."

Charlie pulled off his neck cloth and gave Eric a beseeching glance. "The Waterfall, old fellow."

Eric sighed and stood behind his friend to tie a fresh neck cloth—one of his—around his friend's neck in the required style. Charlie fidgeted and it took three fresh neck cloths before they achieved the desired result. Charlie babbled on about how many children he and Davina would have, and Eric thought that the fair Davina didn't look like the maternal type. She was far too self-centered and too conscious of her elegant figure. He'd known women like that, and child rearing was the last thing on their minds.

"I wish you could go with me, old fellow. Moral support, y'know."

"I'm sure the Lyttons would cause an uproar if I showed my face there. Never cared for me, nor I for them."

"High in the instep. Mrs. Lytton has very little tolerance for anyone on a lower rung on the social ladder, or for undesirables."

Eric had nothing to say to that. "You'll have to make an impression on Miss Davina all by yourself, old fellow."

Charlie began to wring his hands. "What if—?"

"Don't, Charlie. You're only setting yourself up for failure."

Charlie nodded and pinched his mouth into a line of determination.

They went out together. A chilly breeze blew off the Thames. It had been raining intermittently since this morning.

"Good luck, Charlie. I'm going to my club for supper."

Charlie darted off, a complete bundle of nerves. Eric decided to take a detour to Sir Winton's lodgings on foot.

The street was dark and silent, unknown threats waiting in the gloomy doorways, but he moved forward confidently. Fear never walked with him except on that day when Cedric died. It had brought home to him how very close death was every day.

He knocked on Sir Winton's shadowed door, and didn't expect much response. He heard no movement inside. Pounding with his fist, he waited. After an eternity, shuffling sounds came from behind the door, and the door creaked open an inch. He recognized Winton's surly manservant, Yarrow.

"I'm here to see Sir Winton."

"Do you have an appointment?"

Eric shook his head. "Of course not. But I know he's within. I shall not leave until he agrees to see me. If you don't open the door, I'll return here with someone from Bow Street."

The threat had the desired effect. Muttering under his breath, the servant opened the door, and Eric walked into the dank, foul-smelling corridor. A candle burned at one end, and the door to Sir Winton's bed-chamber stood open. The stench grew stronger as Eric moved closer, and he wished he had brought aromatics to press to his nose.

The man lay in bed, the sheets in tatters and the bedcover stained with food. The pillows were gray and soiled.

Eric bent down and stared at the still face. The man was barely breathing. "Winton," Eric shouted. "Can you hear me?" He sensed that the end was near, and he hoped to obtain some kind of confession from the man.

"Devil take you, Ramsdell," the sick man croaked.

"He may take you first," Eric replied. "I visited an old friend of yours, Minette Sharp in Ropehill. She has a very good memory of the day Cedric Brigham died. She's privy to all the details, the note, the meeting, the missing weapon. She's willing to speak with Bow Street," Eric lied, but he hoped to force Sir Winton to confess.

"Rubbish! She knows nothing," the other man wheezed, and Eric took a step back, momentarily nau-seated.

"She will testify. If you don't want to die in prison, you'll confess to one person—Cedric's sister, or to his brother. You would not go to your grave with such guilt on your shoulders. You must atone."

"Nonsense! Cedric died as he lived, recklessly. Had nothing to do with me."

"Your finger pulled the trigger, and you know it. A young man who had his entire life ahead of him lost everything—at your hand."

Sir Winton muttered something under his breath and fell silent.

"I shall bring Mrs. Andrews, Cedric's sister, here tomorrow, and you will confess. I'll make you confess if it's the last thing I ever do."

Sir Winton cackled. "You're a fool, Ramsdell. You always were. Why should I have to humiliate myself and confess to a crime I did not commit?"

"Stop the lying!" Eric bellowed. "Have you no pride, man? No sense of honor?"

The ensuing silence seemed filled with a malevolent presence, and Eric knew it was the hatred that Sir Winton had nurtured over time. He hated everyone.

"At least do one good thing in your life, Winton!"

The man turned his face toward the wall, and Eric had never felt more frustrated. It was no use. Winton would take the truth to his grave, and Eric's life would remain in suspension. Winton had not cared before, so why would he begin to care now?

Eric stormed out of the room. The servant stared at him from the shadows, and Eric suspected he was capable of stabbing him in the back if need be.

"Don't come back here," he rasped.

"Ha! I'll be back with a Bow Street runner. If you're afraid for your own skin, leave now."

"Someone has to feed the master."

"The master is on the threshold of hell. He won't last the week."

Eric left, slamming the door shut behind him. He had threatened to sic a Bow Street runner upon Winton. He had nothing to lose by bringing a runner here, if he could convince them of the necessity. Perhaps Minette would come to his aid, but he doubted it. She could at least testify that Winton had been at Ropehill the day Cedric died. It would also be easy to prove that Cedric had won Winton's fortune at cards, giving the man a motive for murder.

Agitated, he marched through the streets and returned home rather than going to one of the clubs, as he had planned. He *would* bring Lenore to see Sir Winton, come hell or high water. If she believed him, she would be more inclined to accept him into her life. It was all that mattered.

That is, if Ludbank had left the picture, which Eric highly doubted. If he got wind of her continued association with Eric, the man would demand to fight another duel. How tiresome.

All he wanted was to clear his name so that he could live in peace.

In Berkely Square he came across his grandfather stepping into the carriage. "My boy, why don't you dine with me at my club tonight?"

Eric obeyed, as he had planned to go out all along.

His grandfather belonged to the Derby, an ancient and obscure club where most members were over seventy. It suited Eric perfectly, as no one would remember to snub him.

Over a bowl of beef broth, he told his grandfather everything, including his tender feelings for Lenore Andrews.

"My boy! I'm delighted to hear that you've fallen for a woman at last. That'll be the thing that sets your course straight. Nothing like the patter of small feet to keep you on the straight and narrow."

"Grandfather, first I have to clear my name."

"Hmm," the older man said and spooned some more broth into his mouth. "I'll ask old Bolly the judge to accompany you when next you visit Winton. And I'll go too if that makes you feel better."

Eric thought about it for a moment. "Yes . . . of course, but it's Mrs. Andrews I worry about."

"We can bring her too."

"It's not that simple, Grandfather."

"We'll bring that impossible brother of hers as well. The more the merrier."

"Sir Winton will never admit to all these people—"

"Not to worry, lad. I can be very persuasive, my boy."

Eric was filled with frustration, and he highly doubted that his grandfather would find a way where he himself had failed.

"Now find that Miss Sharp and bring her to London tonight. Money will speak with her."

"Yes."

"Since we know some more details, it is high time we rallied 'round you, Eric."

He could only pray that his grandfather knew what he was doing.

Lenore had been invited to the Lyttons's and didn't particularly look forward to the gathering. Mrs. Lytton was a busybody of the worst kind, but she knew Lady Blythe, and that lady had been invited as well. Lenore longed to speak with Eric's grandmother to see if there was something she could do to help the situation.

The Lytton residence was ablaze with candles in all the crystal chandeliers and the windows. The carriage pulled into a small courtyard, and Lenore got out, her hand resting on Charlie's arm. He was trembling with excitement, and she worried that he would make a complete fool of himself at Miss Davina's feet.

Fresh pink roses adorned every vase and urn on the tables in the foyer. Mrs. Lytton wore a plum silk gown with a matching turban that glittered with jewels. Her husband looked distinguished in black evening clothes and a yellow silk waistcoat that strained across his fat middle. Fobs and chains shone in the light from the many candles.

Miss Bright wore a pale pink gown with three tiers of flounces and ribbons and roses threaded through her hair arrangement.

"There she is," Charlie whispered, evidently breathless with excitement.

The object of his adoration fluttered her fan and paid no attention to Charlie. He immediately put on a bored expression as if to convince Davina that he was indifferent about her royal self.

Lenore was ready to scream with annoyance, and she marched forward to greet their hostess. Mrs. Lytton took both her hands and squeezed them until Lenore flinched. "I am so glad you could come. I've invited Sir Charles's nephew as well."

Lenore looked through the open doors to the dining room and noticed a cluster of men around a table that held bottles and glasses. Ricky brayed with laughter, a bright peacock in a sky blue coat among the more somber guests. He also wore a pink-striped satin waistcoat that made him look like a Hogarth caricature.

"Ricky is here," Lenore said to Charlie, who had difficulty tearing his gaze away from Davina.

"That nephew of mine is turning out to be a thorn in my side," Charlie said between clenched teeth.

"He can't help it that Davina showed interest in him."

"But he should stay out of my way," Charlie said with an edge in his voice. "I'll have to tell him as much."

Lenore placed a restraining hand on his arm. "I don't think that would be wise. Young people are apt to do exactly the opposite of what you tell them."

Charlie pursed his lips, looking more agitated by the minute. "You're right, of course, but how do I keep him away from Davina?"

"You can't. If he wants to court her, there's nothing you can do about it, except lock him up in a room with only bread and water."

Charlie rubbed his chin. "That's a thought."

"Don't be ridiculous! He's your own nephew, and you wish him well."

"Mostly." Charlie stalked off to join the men, and she noticed him elbowing Ricky aside rather brusquely. *This has to end,* she thought.

She looked at Davina, who caught her glance and smiled. Perhaps she could do some digging into the matter. She went to greet the younger woman. "You look excessively lovely this evening, Davina."

"Just an old dress I pulled out of the armoire," the younger woman lied nonchalantly.

Lenore was certain the creation was new. It looked as if it had arrived that day from the modiste, which was probably closer to the truth. "The gentlemen will fall all over themselves to give you compliments."

Davina fluttered her fan and sighed. "They are all complete bores."

"Hmm, does no one hold your interest? The Season is just about over; I would think you have some serious admirers."

Davina gave the group of men in the other room a

look full of exasperation. "Nincompoops, the lot of them."

"I see." Lenore's spirits sank. It looked as if Charlie didn't have much of a chance with Davina, and Lenore had known it in her heart. "Charlie is a wonderful man. I've known him for a number of years."

"Not enough money there," Davina said with her nose in the air. She walked off, and Lenore resented her high-handed ways. Charlie was the fortunate one if Davina ignored him, though he wouldn't see it that way. He would survive the rejection.

The evening progressed, and she noticed Davina simpering over Ricky, who had a pot of money coming to him upon his father's death, Lenore thought. Charlie wore a thunderous expression all evening, and he barely touched the rack of lamb and tiny potatoes served, or the peas. He only drank glass after glass of wine, and Lenore whispered to him to stop making a fool of himself.

She thought he would get up at one point and challenge his nephew to a duel over the heartless Davina, who did everything to provoke every male in the company. Ricky looked rather pleased with himself, and Lenore prayed that Charlie would see the true character of his beloved.

A dessert of sponge cake dipped in brandy and covered with whipped cream and raisins came as a grand finish to the meal, but Charlie left his untouched.

After the meal, as the ladies left for the drawing room, Davina excused herself and went to primp. The men had already sampled more brandy in the dining room than was prudent. Ricky disappeared—to ease his bladder, no doubt, Lenore thought as she saw him slinking down the dark corridor.

Half an hour passed and Ricky still hadn't returned, and neither had Davina. Another hour passed and Charlie came out of the dining room and inquired about his missing nephew. He went in search of him and returned with a hastily scribbled note.

Davina's chaperone, Mrs. Millspoon, stood as he waved the note about. "Where is my charge? Davina went upstairs to lie down for a few minutes. She complained about a headache."

"Gone with Ricky, no doubt. The pair has eloped," Charlie shouted, beside himself with wrath.

Mrs. Millspoon fainted dead away, and Lenore started waving a vinaigrette under her nose. She then placed a pillow under the older woman's head to make her more comfortable. *Damned young fool,* she thought. Ricky had planned to elope all along. Why else had he hurried away like a thief in the night?

And Davina—why would she slink away? The girl could have anyone she wished, and she ran off with a youth barely out of the schoolroom, ruining her reputation in the process. There was no understanding human nature, Lenore thought.

"I'll never be able to show my face again," Mrs. Millspoon moaned.

"There, there, we don't know the whole of it yet. Perhaps there is some misunderstanding," Lenore said.

"Never! Oh, the ungrateful minx," Mrs. Millspoon wailed and fainted once more.

Chapter 19

Charlie suffered the torment of the betrayal. His anger with Ricky raged as Lenore took him home after the disastrous dinner. "Now you see the real Davina. She pretended that no one was good enough for her, yet she decides to elope with that foolish nephew of yours. You can no longer ignore her immaturity."

"No," Charlie said forlornly, "but my feelings have not diminished."

Lenore wanted to hit him with one of the pillows in the carriage. "Of all the silly absurdities—"

Charlie glared at her. "No more foolish than the feelings you harbor for Eric."

"I don't—"

"Don't lie to me! I've seen how you look at him, and he at you. Have I berated you for your weakness? No. I have supported you."

Lenore could not find anything to say to that. Charlie was right.

One couldn't help the emotions that arose when the man one cared about entered the room. "At least Eric is not a twit like Davina. You deserve much better, Charlie."

The man groaned and buried his face in his hands. "I shall ride after them and challenge Ricky."

"It is up to Davina's relatives to charge ahead."

"I am responsible for Ricky. I've cared for that pup since he came down from Oxford, and look how he repays me. He shall pay for his arrogance."

"Revenge is pointless."

When she had come to, Mrs. Millspoon told them that Ricky had offered for Davina's hand, and Mr. Millspoon had flatly refused to give his permission. Clearly the old man was holding out for a marquess or a viscount with deep pockets.

"Mr. Bright will have Ricky's head on a platter, and he's welcome to it," Charlie said.

Lenore sighed heavily. She was immensely tired of the spectacle, and she wished Charlie would come to his senses. "Davina wholly ignored you tonight. Doesn't that mean something? She showed no interest in you. In fact, she went as far as to call all gentlemen in the room nincompoops."

"You just don't want me to be happy," Charlie said in a gloomy voice.

"Nonsense! I wish you nothing but happiness—with a woman who has something besides cotton wool between her ears."

Charlie sighed theatrically. "Davina has no cotton wool—"

"No, *she* has sawdust between her ears."

"You are very cruel, Lenore."

Lenore drew a sigh of relief when the coach stopped at her house and Charlie escorted her inside. She prayed he would take himself off before she said something that might ruin their friendship. He seemed unable to make a decision, but then he recalled his plan to ride after the elopers and regained some of his vigor. He made a hasty retreat before Lenore could argue.

"What a dreadful night," Lenore said to herself as she slipped off the embroidered fringed shawl she'd used as a wrap.

She slept badly that night, dreaming of bolting horses that trampled everything in their way. She also remembered dreaming about Eric Ramsdell right before she awakened. He'd been beckoning her to come to him, deep longing in his eyes. Her own longing had been ignited, and she wondered if she would ever forget his face.

Aaron Knapp, the Bow Street runner, wrinkled his nose as he and Eric entered Sir Winton's lodgings. A man was coming out of the sickroom as they walked down the corridor, and he looked thunderous.

"Can we help you?" Eric offered.

"Unless you can pay his rent in arrears, I doubt it," the man said icily.

"Oh. You must be the beleaguered landlord."

"The snake has not paid me anything for six months, and I've tried to have him put in a hospital, but he threatens to shoot me if I move him." He rolled the brim of his hat between his hands. "I'm not a heartless man, and it's clear to see that Sir Winton is dying, but he's nastier than an adder, and I could rent these lodgings for profit."

Eric introduced himself and the Bow Street runner. "We might be able to help in that regard."

"Bow Street? What has Sir Winton done?"

"That's what we're trying to discover," Mr. Knapp said. "I have some questions for him."

The landlord brightened. "I won't object if you take him to Newgate Prison."

Eric entered the sickroom, and Sir Winton looked flushed and angry. "I heard that last statement," he said to the landlord. "No one is going to move me from here."

Mr. Knapp sat on the only chair by the bed and introduced himself. He pulled out a book and a quill, and set up an inkhorn on the nightstand, among all the bottles of medicine.

"I told you I would be back," Eric said. "Even as we speak, Minette Sharp is giving a statement to another runner. We have proved that you were at Ropehill the day Cedric died, and that you were seen at the Red Pheasant as you delivered a note to a young boy who could not be found again."

The sick man lifted his shoulders and coughed. "So what? I am free to go where I please."

"Is it true that you once were a wealthy man and that Mr. Cedric Brigham won your fortune at the card tables?" the runner asked.

Sir Winton gave a reluctant nod. "It is no secret. He stole my money, more or less."

"Gambling is unfortunate," the runner continued. "It does give you a motive for wanting to see him dead. Revenge is sweet."

"Cedric was a fool, but you shall have to prove I killed him, Mr. Knapp. I know you can't."

"Are you willing to die with that on your conscience?" the runner asked. "You deserve to burn in Hell. You need to pray for forgiveness, man, and you need to receive absolution."

Sir Winton cackled. "I'm damned certain Cedric didn't feel any repentance when he died. He was a thief and proud of it." He fell into a coughing fit that wracked his thin frame. Eric felt increasingly nause-ated from the stench in the room.

"You shall be punished once we have proof of your guilt," the runner said. "An innocent man should not suffer the consequences of something you did."

Sir Winton looked uncomfortable for a moment, but the glance he gave Eric was full of hatred. "You'll get no confession out of me. You're wasting your time."

"I never did anything to you, Winton. Why the hatred?"

"You are alive and I must die. Why should you have everything when I have nothing left?"

"You're highly mistaken on that score! Because of you, my life has been in a shambles, and I lost a dear friend."

"Good! You don't deserve to have what you have. Your arrogance hurt everyone close to you."

"That may have been true at one time in my life, but I've learned my lesson. Cedric's death brought home the uselessness of my existence, and I've found some purpose that will serve to help others." He nod-ded at the sick man. "I shall endeavor to get you the best treatment."

"There's no cure for consumption." Sir Winton continued to cough. "I shan't confess."

The Bow Street runner looked at Eric, who made a grimace. Sir Winton would not give an inch, and Eric's only hope was Minette Sharp, but she had not witnessed the shooting. They left the room, and the landlord said, "I wouldn't put it past the man to murder someone. I wish you would just throw him into gaol."

The Bow Street runner, a man of great patience, said, "We can't throw someone in prison due to hearsay."

"I shall find some proof!" the landlord promised. He put on his hat and left the building.

"That would be helpful," the runner said with a sigh. "As it is, we have nothing."

Eric couldn't recall a time when he felt more frustrated. "We have to find something that will prove his guilt."

"A witness would be just the thing."

Eric knew he had no chance of finding one at this juncture. He'd tried everything in the past. If only the matter could be resolved so that he could approach Lenore as a free man. As it was, she was as unattainable as the moon.

He longed for her with every fiber of his being.

The Bow Street runner looked at him with suspicion. "This may be a hopeless case, Mr. Ramsdell. I'm only doing this as a favor to your grandfather."

Eric nodded. "I'm well aware of that. I don't want to waste your time."

"Find a witness, and I'll be back to arrest Sir Winton. He doesn't seem long for this world anyway."

"I want to prove my innocence before he dies, or I'll never be exonerated."

"Yes, I can see your point. We can keep hammering him with questions until he tires and confesses."

"Someone saw a small boy with Sir Winton at the Red Pheasant the day Cedric died. If only I could get my hands on him."

The runner nodded. "Aye, that would be helpful— very helpful indeed."

Eric didn't want to leave, but he couldn't remain here. It was fruitless to badger the sick man. There would be no overcoming Winton's stubbornness, Eric thought. He would deny everything with his last breath . . . He didn't want to finish the thought.

The next afternoon, Lenore was going over the books with her accountant in her study. Her affairs were in order. She had inherited the bulk of Ronald's estate, but he'd settled an enormous sum on the woman who had mothered his children.

Lenore had felt great pain every time the numbers had been explained to her, but now she found she didn't care much anymore. She was free of the anger and the anguish, and she thought that was some kind of victory.

"Someone's at the door," the accountant said and looked up.

A knock sounded, and Charlie stepped inside, bedraggled. Evidently he hadn't changed clothes since last night. His face had a red, mottled look, as if he'd been running, and he breathed hard. "Lenore!"

There was no sign of Beaton. She led Charlie out to the foyer and then into one of the parlors and closed the door. "What is going on?"

"I rode after them as I said I would. Caught up with them outside of Northampton, and they had not rested. On their way to Gretna Green, don't you know."

"We suspected as much since they eloped. Were they unharmed?"

"Aye, unscathed and nestled in the carriage like two lovebirds."

"That could be expected as well." Lenore patted Charlie's hand as he sat beside her on the settee. She rang the bell and ordered some tea from Beaton.

"Davina could have had anyone. Now her reputation is in shreds."

Lenore nodded. "She is foolish as well as selfish."

"My heart is broken," he said with a trembling voice. "She screeched at me like a washerwoman and said the most wounding things. She said I had no style, that I was a bore, that no one would ever marry me because I have an ugly nose. She even said she hated the way I walked, like a duck. No woman in her right mind would consider a future with me because my friends were criminals and hangers-on, my women friends old sharp-tongued harpies."

"Dear me," Lenore said and patted his shoulder. "You must be very angry."

"I'm so angry I could explode! The nerve of that . . . that doxy!"

"Yes . . . I suppose your more tender feelings are, well, no more?"

"Right you are! I finally saw her true nature, and I consider myself fortunate to have escaped her. Not so Ricky. He's going to have to listen to her harangues forever."

Lenore worried about that, as Ricky was no match for the calculating Miss Bright. "We shall hope that she tires of him and gives him his congé. Perhaps something will happen on the way to Scotland."

"Ricky is not up to snuff. He has no experience with women, and one like this least of all."

Lenore said a silent prayer that Ricky would be freed of the woman's claws as well.

Charlie leaned his head in his hands, just as she'd seen him do so many times before. There has to come a time when life gets better, she thought, and patted his shoulder once more. "The tea will cheer you up.

I'm sure Cook will send up some of her ginger cake as well. You know how much you like that."

Lenore was exhausted from the swell of emotion. Charlie brightened somewhat after the tea and cake, and he said he was going home to write to Ricky's mother—his sister—to inform her of the disaster that had occurred.

"Do be sure to get some rest, Charlie."

Later that day she received a note from Charlie, who wrote that Ricky had returned after convincing Davina that elopement was no more than cheating oneself and one's family of a joyous wedding. There would be plenty of time, he'd stated. Very perceptive of the greenhorn, Charlie had added.

Miss Bright had then claimed she had no real interest in Ricky; she had only wanted to make Lord Ludbank jealous. And Ludbank wasn't even at the dinner party, Charlie continued. Ludbank had heard about it and sworn off women forever, especially after realizing he would never have a chance to win Lenore's heart.

Lenore was grateful for Ludbank's denunciation of women. He would leave her alone from now on. Miss Bright had been packed off to the country, where she now had to ponder her stupidity and hope to ensnare the local vicar into matrimony.

No one in London wanted her. The news had traveled through the *haute monde* like wildfire.

What a strange turn of events, Lenore thought. Davina Bright had had the world at her feet, and thrown it away in a fit of pique, trampling two gentlemen who had done nothing but adore her. It was the outside of enough! Such selfishness and such contempt could not be matched. At least Charlie and Ricky had been spared.

She had heard nothing from Eric Ramsdell; and, according to Charlie, nothing had changed. Eric was no closer to solving his problems, and she anticipated no solution to the dilemma. She saw no future with him, but she could not shake off the thoughts that revolved around him.

She was becoming as afflicted as Charlie had been. Blushing, she remembered the kisses she had shared with Eric and knew she could never forget him, no matter what happened in the future. Why was love so difficult?

She decided to write a note to him. Beaton knocked on the door as she pulled out a sheet of paper and her quill.

"Ma'am, this was outside." He held out the diary, and by the guilty look on his face she knew he'd not been able to discover the identity of the secret correspondent.

She received it without comment. Beaton left, closing the door softly behind him. The entry was lengthy, and she read it, noting the good wishes at the end. She would not hear from him again. A keen sense of loss filled her, as if a good friend had left her life and gone across the sea with no promise that they would ever meet again.

She wished she knew his identity. Her correspondent had turned from adamant opponent into trusted friend; someone she'd felt comfortable enough with to confide her deepest thoughts. "Drat it all," she said out loud and began to write her note.

* * *

Eric needed no excuse to visit Lenore, not after he received her missive full of yearning. He knocked on her door and carried one perfect red rose, which he handed to her. "For your beauty, inside and out," he said and kissed her hand.

She held her breath and admired the rose. Pressing the dewy petals to her nose, she inhaled the heady fragrance. "Thank you," she whispered.

"I missed you," he said, "but I should not be here."

"And let me suffer as well?" she asked.

He groaned and swept her into his arms. Holding her hard, he whispered. "How can this be? Why are we separated?"

"You know the answer."

"I have a confession to make," he said. "I doubt I can free myself from the burden of guilt, but I'm doing my best."

"How can I help?" she asked against his shirtfront. She belonged here, she thought, as he held her tightly against his chest.

"Would you care to help?" he whispered.

"Of course. I want this mystery solved as much as you do."

"Would you come with me to Sir Winton's lodgings? If only he would admit his guilt. He may speak with you where I've failed at every turn. I warn you, however, he's filthy."

"I don't care. Let's go now." She swept out of the room and fetched her shawl, bonnet, and gloves.

Eric watched her leave the room and his heart contracted with the love he felt. Never had he expected to feel so deeply for anyone. Hope for their success shone on the horizon, but they still had obstacles to overcome. Besides, how could he live with the deception of the diary?

He had no answer to that. Later, he would confess, when they'd solved the problem with Sir Winton and actually had a future together.

His carriage rode over the cobbles, and they sat silently in the dark interior interior, gazing at each other.

"This has to work," she said. "He must be made to confess."

"If you knew Sir Winton you'd understand you can't force him into anything."

She nodded. "I realize no one wants to confess to murder, especially if someone else has taken the blame."

He heaved an audible sigh. The carriage turned toward Haymarket and down a narrow, dark alley.

"We're here," Eric said when the carriage stopped. He helped her down, and she wrinkled her nose at the stench of mud and refuse in the street. Eric knocked on the door, and the surly servant opened it. Without speaking, Eric made his way into the darkened hallway and led Lenore down it. His heart hammered uncomfortably. What if Sir Winton would not cooperate? *How much more must I suffer?* Eric thought.

The familiar stench met them, and Eric pushed the door to the sickroom open. To his surprise, he saw that Sir Winton had visitors. Minette Sharp and a small boy stood by the bed, and he overheard a statement before Minette noticed their presence. "You never acknowledged poor Tom here, but you used him to set up a murder. Your own son!"

Chapter 20

Your son? Eric couldn't believe his ears. "I didn't know you had a son, Winton," he said as he pushed his way into the room.

Minette flinched back as if slapped. "Eric Ramsdell," she whispered.

"Yes, it's indeed I, and I'm grateful you're in London, Minette. You have come to testify, haven't you?"

"I had a visitor from Bow Street, and they threatened me."

"Shut up, you slut," Sir Winton hissed, his red-rimmed eyes flashing with anger. He followed Eric's progress, and his eyes narrowed as he noticed Lenore. "Who's the fine filly?"

"Mrs. Andrews, Cedric's sister," Eric offered. "She wants to know what really happened to her brother."

"Why would she care? He's beyond pain now," Sir Winton said.

"But we are not," Lenore said. She glanced at Minette. "And I'd wager she's not beyond pain either."

Minette chewed on her lower lip, and the pale boy clung to her skirts.

"And the boy. What are you doing to him?" Lenore asked.

"Doing to him? Nothing. I can't get out of bed." He

coughed as if his lungs would turn themselves inside out, then collapsed against the pillows.

Lenore pulled out a handkerchief from her reticule and wiped her eyes. She was crying softly, and Eric felt a desire to strangle the man in the bed. Lenore sat on the chair by the bed, close enough where the awful man could touch her. She began talking in a low voice, telling everyone about Cedric's childhood, remembering stories that would touch the hardest heart. She went on to recount his years at university and then how he came to London and indulged himself without any sense of responsibility.

"Perhaps it doesn't matter that he's dead. He lived carelessly and without thought for anyone who he might've hurt," Lenore went on. "But he had a good heart underneath it all. He would have changed had he lived. Can't you just honor him by telling me the truth?"

"It's no use appealing to Winton's finer nature. He has none," Eric said in disgust.

"Yes, he does. Everyone does."

Eric snorted, but Lenore took the ailing man's dirty hand and squeezed it. "Please, give me what I'm asking for, Sir Winton. You are already forgiven. All I want is to know the truth."

Eric snorted, but Minette hushed him, and Tom stared at Sir Winton with very large eyes. He looked uncannily like Sir Winton. There was no mistaking the parentage.

"I didn't know you had a child, Minette," Eric said.

"Tom is my everything," she said. "A blessing despite his father."

Eric nodded. "So far unsullied by any dark influences."

Minette looked uncomfortable. "Not quite. The villain has used Tom on occasion. Young legs run faster than old ones."

Eric didn't know what to make of the statement, but he listened to Lenore speaking softly to the sick man, who seemed to be asleep.

"Tell me the truth, oh please," she begged, but the man didn't move.

"Sir Winton, you have nothing to lose," she continued. She shook his hand, but it hung limply in her grip.

Eric had a premonition. "I believe he has passed on," he said and placed his fingertips on the man's filthy neck, seeking a pulse. "He's dead."

Minette shivered and the room seemed darker. Lenore placed the hand of the dead man on the coverlet. She wiped away a tear, defeated at the very end.

"Too late," Minette said, and Eric swore under his breath.

Lenore's eyes flowed over with tears, and she cried silently, pressing her handkerchief to her cheeks. Eric had never felt more helpless.

"'E killed 'im," said the boy suddenly, his high voice sharp in the room. "I wuz there, 'idin'. I gave the man a note from me father to meet 'im in the curve in the road, near the ditch. 'E shot 'im and threw the pistol in th' river."

Not even a breath could be heard in the room. "'E killed 'im. 'E 'ated 'im 'cause 'e took all the money. Father told me so."

Minette shook him. "Are ye lyin', Tom?"

"No, ma. 'E shot 'im dead."

Minette pressed the young boy close. "Ye shouldn't 'ave to see things like that, poor Tom."

"'E gave me 'alf a crown to give that man the note."

Minette stared at the corpse in the bed. "At first he wasn't goin' to acknowledge his own son, but when it got convenient, he did. He was an evil man, and every time I thought I'd gotten rid of him, he found me and tortured me with threats."

Lenore cried softly, and Eric went to her and placed his hand on her shoulder to support her. At least she didn't move away.

"Are you willing to speak with Bow Street and tell them what you told us?" Eric asked Minette.

"Aye, of course. Win is not goin' to get the last word. He'll be punished enough in Hell." She held her boy close. "Tom here will speak of what he knows as well. Yer name will be cleared, Mr. Ramsdell."

She gave him a speculative look, and Eric said a silent prayer of thanks that Minette would help him when he most needed it. She could have chosen to spit in his face, but she didn't. "I can't thank you enough, Minette." He pointed at the boy. "I'll see to it that Tom receives a decent education and an apprenticeship. He's worth his weight in gold, and I hate the idea that he had to suffer as well."

"He's a sturdy boy; he'll be fine. We all live close to death, and some leave this world more violently than others."

"True enough, Minette." Eric pulled the grimy sheet over the dead man's face. Tom hadn't shed one tear for his father. "I shall call in the authorities and make arrangements for a funeral."

Minette nodded, and brought the boy outside. Yarrow, the servant, was skulking in the shadows, and Eric relayed his plan, sensing that the man would be long gone before the authorities arrived.

They walked outside into the damp night. Rain

hung in the air, and the air was still and heavy over the city. Before morning, the city would be shrouded in a dense fog. He assisted Lenore into the carriage. She leaned back against the squabs, and he sat next to her and held her close.

"It is a shame that you had to witness this, but I must admit that I'm elated and relieved," he said.

"Yes . . . you are a free man at last," she said, relief filling her voice. "Wait until I tell Edward."

"Shall we go to Grosvenor Square now? I want his permission to court you properly."

She clapped her hands together. "Yes! Let's find Edward and tell him the truth."

Eric laughed and pounded the hatch to direct the coachman. "I hope he's home."

Edward was sitting in his study, going over financial ledgers, when the butler announced his sister and Eric Ramsdell. With an annoyed flick of his wrist, he closed the ledger at hand and glared at them as they entered the room. "If you've come here to plead, just know I'm turning a deaf ear. You'll receive no leniency from me, and, Lenore, you shall be packed off to the spinster aunts on the morrow."

"I shall do no such thing, Edward."

She walked across the room and sat down on a chair on the other side of the desk and stared at him defiantly. Eric did the same.

"We found a witness to Cedric's murder, a ten-year-old boy named Tom—Sir Winton Niles's illegitimate son."

Edward stared from one to the other. "Is this a cruel joke?"

Eric shook his head. "No, it's not. The mother, Sir

Winton's erstwhile mistress, has information as well, and they are going to speak with Bow Street."

"Dashed if I'll believe this!"

"Truth will out." Eric leaned closer. "Shall we let bygones be bygones? I'd like to court your sister properly."

"I don't see why you have to ask me. She never does anything I suggest, so I'd better stay out of it. Good luck with the contrary baggage! She'll lead you a merry dance if you're so foolish as to marry her."

"I'll take the risk."

Lenore threw her arms around Eric's neck and Edward rolled his eyes heavenward. He stood. "I will leave you two to come to an agreement. Shouldn't take long by the looks of it."

He went out and Lenore looked at Eric with huge eyes.

He was overcome with feeling and his next words tumbled out in a rush. "I haven't loved anyone as much as I love you, Lenore, not since I was a child and loved my dog, Clarence. Not that there's a comparison, mind you. Lud, I scarcely know how to explain—"

Her gaze narrowed and she stiffened visibly. "What was the dog's name? Clarence?"

He nodded, wondering why she had changed so much in the course of a breath. "Yes, Clarence. My faithful companion—"

She pointed a gloved finger at him and anger flared in her eyes. "You're the one who has been writing in my journal all this time!"

Blast and damn! He shrunk inside, knowing there was no way out but to tell the truth. He nodded, swearing at himself silently. "I did."

"You were never going to tell me, were you?"

He squirmed in his seat. "If you read the last entry, you know I intended to close the chapter."

"You wrote all those unfeeling things to me." Her voice trembled with anger.

He nodded. "Yes, but then I changed—"

"You knew who I was all along."

He grimaced. "I found the diary when you forgot it under your chair at the Rose Tearoom. It was only meant as a lark. At the time, I had no one to turn to, and I thought it might be entertaining to correspond with you, but I never dreamed you would reply."

"How could you?" Big tears started rolling down her cheeks, and he bent forward to wipe them away, but she smacked his hand away.

"It was foolish, but I learned so much from you. When I had no hope, you gave me some, and you taught me about love. Before you, I understood very little. I know what I did was unforgivable, but I didn't mean to cause you any harm."

"But you led me along blindly. If you hadn't slipped with Clarence's name just now, I doubt you'd ever have told me the truth. You made a fool out of me!"

"I did not," Eric protested. "You essentially agreed to the charade by replying."

"Because I could not stand by and encourage such rampant arrogance by my silence."

"M'dear, you cut me down to size, and I'm grateful for it," he said. He wiped his hand across his brow, suddenly exhausted. He stood. "I'm going to take you home, Lenore. I understand if you never want to speak to me again."

She rose without a word and led the way out into the hallway. There was no sign of Edward or any servant, so they let themselves out. Neither one spoke on the way to Lenore's house, and Eric felt that he had gained and lost something priceless in one day.

"I don't expect you to believe me, but I had planned to confess about the diary once my name had been cleared. There was a chance that would never happen."

She didn't reply, and he left her at her home on Albemarle Street.

Chapter 21

Eric didn't sleep for days. He heard nothing from Lenore. He set up lodgings in London for Minette and her son and arranged for domestic employment for her. At last Cedric could rest in peace, and Eric was immensely grateful for that.

A week after Lenore found out about the diary, he purchased another one just like it and wrote the most touching confession of love.

Dearest Lenore,

In this somewhat anonymous manner it's easy to open my heart and show you what is in it. All shyness falls away and I declare a love for you I never thought possible. You've given me the gift of understanding, taught me to take the time to really see another person. I pray you will give me a second chance to prove my true feelings for you. I shall be eternally sorry for my behavior—and know that I disliked the idea of deceiving you, but once I had taken the plunge, it was most difficult to admit to such blatant subterfuge. You would have been very angry—as you were when you discovered the truth. In due time, I might have confessed, but I might have waited until you had my ring on your finger.

*More than anything, I want you to be my wife and
I promise that I'll never keep anything from you in the
future. Please believe me as you gave me the benefit of
the doubt in the case of Cedric's death. I'm not a de-
ceitful person at heart, only foolish. I love you more
than life itself—please marry me.*

Wrapping the diary up as a present, he had it delivered to Lenore's address with a large bouquet of
red roses.

He didn't hear back from her, and his spirits
plunged. Charlie, who had miraculously recovered
from his heartbreak, couldn't cheer him with his
good humor, and he claimed that Lenore was just as
blue-deviled as Eric.

"You two must resolve this. You were excessively
addle-brained, Eric, but I understand your reasoning.
I'm certain you'll both wither away if you do not
marry the woman."

A week later, Eric received the diary, and his heart
sank. She had returned it. But to his surprise, there
was an entry. Her handwriting didn't seem the same;
it was shaky and weak.

I forgive you, and yes, I want to marry you.

Eric whooped with joy. He'd never dressed so quickly,
and ten minutes later he rushed over to Albemarle
Street and knocked on her door. Beaton looked at him
with disapproval.

"Is Mrs. Andrews at home?"

"Yes, she is, but I doubt she wants to see you, Mr.
Ramsdell."

"She does," he said and stormed past the disapproving butler. Flinging open the doors, he found Lenore at the breakfast table. Her eyes were huge in her pale face and looked even larger when she saw Eric.

"What in the world—?"

He lifted her up from her chair and her rose gown swirled around her legs as he swung her around. "We will be married just as soon as I can procure a special license."

"What?"

"Married." He set her down and stared at her intently.

"Have you gone mad?" She stared at him in outrage.

Eric stopped in midstride and dropped his hands from her waist. "You wrote that you agreed to marry me."

"I did no such thing!"

Wordlessly, he brought out the diary and showed her. "I didn't write that," she said.

"Charlie," they said in unison.

"Damn the man," Eric said and sat down and buried his head in his hands.

Silence hung in the room, and he feared she would storm out, but she stayed where he'd put her down.

"He thought it would be important for us to talk," she said.

He nodded. "I meant every word I wrote in the diary, Lenore. Shall we start another journal? One with only love letters?"

She stared at him for the longest time. "Yes . . . very well. I accept. I will marry you, because I can't face a life without you."

He wasn't sure he'd heard right, but he got up and gathered her into his arms. He would never let her go now. "I love you," he whispered against her hair. "More than I can ever write in one journal. I need a dozen."

She laughed. "Dear Eric . . . I love you too."

More Regency Romance From Zebra